A DEODORIZER
OF DEAD DOGS

Satiric Tales
by Ambrose Bierce

OTHER BOOKS IN THE GREAT STUFF
YOU NEVER READ IN SCHOOL SERIES:

Fart Proudly
(The Humorous Writings of Benjamin Franklin)

A DEODORIZER OF DEAD DOGS

Another Collection Of Great Stuff
You Never Read In School—
Satires & Tall Tales

by Ambrose Bierce

Edited by Carl Japikse

ENTHEA PRESS
Atlanta, Georgia

Contents

Introduction

Ambrose Bierce may well be the best American author you have never read—or even heard about. Were he a well-known figure, he would probably be referred to as "the American Swift," comparing him to Irish satirist Jonathan Swift. But he is not, so the tribute remains unechoed.

In my youth, I attended a fine public school and went on to graduate, with honors in the study of English literature, from an outstanding Eastern college. I specialized in studying the dark art of satire. In the course of these studies, I read widely and voraciously. I consumed more Russian novels than I could stomach; I devoured Trollope and Sterne and Fielding in a single gulp. Yet in all of these excursions into the realm of literature, both enforced and voluntary, I was never once introduced to the brilliance of Ambrose Bierce.

This omission is not an indictment of Bierce, but rather of the lack of imagination and taste in modern American education. Education is supposed to preserve the reputation of great writers such as Bierce, and make us aware of them. Instead, it has consigned Bierce to a black hole of oblivion.

Why is that? It is always hard to discern what goes on in the thin mind of modern American education, but my guess is that the antipathy and disregard that has been shown Bierce is just another example of rank discrimination and bias. In other words, the poobahs of modern literature do not like him. They regard him as a nasty person who did despicable things and wrote about horrible topics that no teacher or professor wants to be questioned about. One of Bierce's favorite literary devices, after all, was death—usually a bizarre, exaggerated, and painful form of death. Academia just is not prepared to cope. So it ignores what it does not understand, and hopes it will go away.

But it can't—and it won't. Bierce is too good an author to be consigned to the dung heaps. He keeps resurrecting himself in the most unusual ways.

My first introduction to Ambrose Bierce was some twenty years ago, when I read a novella by Robert Heinlein, the well-known science fiction author, called *Lost Legacy*. In this story, a group of university professors, searching in the Sierra Madre mountains, encounter Bierce, still alive after all of these years. Instead of dying, Bierce, who was profoundly attracted to the supernatural in his writings, had joined a community of advanced recluses who had learned the secret of everlasting life.

In writing this novella, Heinlein was playing off of the mystery that surrounded Bierce's final days. As a man in his seventies, Bierce headed to Mexico, purportedly to report on the insurrection of Pancho Villa. At this point, he disappeared and was never heard from again. Speculation has raged for a whole century: did he die en route? Did he actually reach Pancho Villa's camp, only to die in battle—or to be executed by the *guerrillero* himself, as the result, perhaps, of an ill-timed insult? Or did he stage his disappearance so that he could go into retirement from civilized life? No one knows.

Normally, this kind of mystery enhances an author's reputation. Bierce, however, did not benefit in this way. The Moral Minority of professional education saw its opportunity and passed judgment: Ambrose Bierce was no Jonathan Swift—not even an American version of him.

I have a theory why this judgment occurred. All truly great satirists run the risk of being disliked by thin-minded people, because they poke fun at the smudged corners of human hypocrisy. Swift did this brilliantly—and so did Bierce. But Jonathan Swift had a redeeming feature that Ambrose Bierce lacked. Swift was a dean in the Catholic church. His morality was therefore religious as well as sarcastic. Bierce, on the other hand, was a journalist and a notorious rogue. Therefore, his satire could hardly be anything more than the ravings of a demented mind. Case closed. Memo to all educators: do not include any Ambrose Bierce stories, even the harmless ones, in anthologies. He is a black goat of American literature—a black scapegoat, that is.

It does not matter that Swift was even more outrageous than Bierce. Whereas Bierce treats murder as a commonplace, acceptable solution to life's problems—tongue in cheek, of course—Swift, with the same anatomical obstruction, modestly proposes the sale of the butchered babies of the poor to serve as food for the banquet tables of the rich!

I believe the two of them are cut from the same satirical cloth, and need to be read by every literate person. Swift already is, at least in a minimalist way: most educated people have read something by him, some time. Bierce, on the other hand, needs to be restored, with fanfare, to the anthologies our students read in school.

After all, who could read "A Revolt of the Gods" or "My Favorite Murder" without deciding that American literature might be fun, after all?

The stories that are included in this collection are mostly ones that Bierce described as "tall tales." Tall tales are a story form indigenous to the American West of the 19th century. Bierce took this story form and converted it into a literary form—a literary form especially suited for satire and dark humor.

Satire makes its point by taking the small and petty hypocrisies of life and exaggerating them out of proportion—or by taking a great and important issue and shrinking it down to pettiness.

Bierce found the tall tale exquisitely suited to this task. The whole point of a tall tale is that it exaggerates the truth. No sober person has ever truly believed that Pecos Bill could actually ride a tornado.

But in the tall tale tradition of the West, he did, and still does.

In Bierce's hands, this same form of exaggeration allows him to create societies in which a nephew who murders his universally hated uncle is applauded instead of condemned, especially since he executes the deed with such bravado and spirit.

This does not imply that Bierce favored chaos or mayhem. It simply means that he used such controversial topics as death and murder to examine our social and cultural assumptions about life—and poke fun at the inconsistencies.

As these stories reveal, Bierce wrote with razor sharp insight into the motives and morals of most human beings. These stories are not just fun to read, but are also peepholes into our secret foibles and follies. This inner depth may not be obvious at first, but it is there. Keep looking for it, and you will find it. For those who are not accustomed to reading satire, a clue might help. In most of these stories, Bierce tips his hand as to the true object of his satire only in the last paragraph or so. In the first story, for instance, it is not until the final sentence that it becomes fully clear that Bierce is satirizing the use of blackmail and confrontation by the labor movement.

In that story, by the way, the narrator ends by identifiying himself as the Chief of Misrule. This is actually an ancient title dating back hundreds of years to England, based in a tradition somewhat akin to our modern conception of April Fool. The Chief of Misrule is someone appointed to poke fun at all hypocrisy, high or low, and is exempt from any repercussions.

This is the role Bierce himself plays as author of these fine satires—these tall tales.

Read them and enjoy them. Then decide for yourself: wouldn't English class have been a whole lot more fun reading these stories instead of *Silas Marner?* Or even Ernest Hemingway?

—Carl Japikse

A DEODORIZER
OF DEAD DOGS

A REVOLT OF THE GODS

My father was a deodorizer of dead dogs, my mother kept the only shop for the sale of cats'-meat in my native city. They did not live happily; the difference in social rank was a chasm which could not be bridged by the vows of marriage. It was indeed an ill-assorted and most unlucky alliance; and as might have been foreseen it ended in disaster. One morning after the customary squabbles at breakfast, my father rose from the table, quivering and pale with wrath, and proceeding to the parsonage thrashed the clergyman who had performed the marriage ceremony. The act was generally condemned and public feeling ran so high against the offender that people would permit dead dogs to lie on their property until the fragrance was deafening rather than employ him; and the municipal authorities suffered one bloated old mastiff to utter itself from a public square in so clamorous an exhalation that passing strangers supposed themselves to be in the vicinity of a sawmill. My father was indeed unpopular. During these dark days the family's sole dependence was on my mother's emporium for cats'-meat.

The business was profitable. In that city, which was the oldest in the world, the cat was an object of veneration. Its worship was the religion of the country. The multiplication and addition of cats were a perpetual instruction in arithmetic. Naturally, any inattention to the wants of a cat was punished with great severity in this world and the next; so my good mother numbered her patrons by the hundred. Still, with an unproductive husband and seventeen children she had some difficulty in making both ends cats'-meat; and at last the necessity of increasing the discrepancy between the cost price and the selling price of her carnal wares drove her to an expedient which proved eminently disastrous: she conceived the unlucky notion of retaliating by refusing to sell cats'-meat until the boycott was taken off her husband.

On the day when she put this resolution into practice the shop was thronged with excited customers, and others extended in turbulent and restless masses up four streets, out of sight. Inside there was nothing but cursing, crowding, shouting and menace. Intimidation was freely resorted to—several of my younger brothers and sisters being threatened with cutting up for the cats—but my mother was as firm as a rock, and the day was a black one for Sardasa, the ancient and sacred city that was the scene of these events. The lock-out was vigorously maintained, and seven hundred and fifty thousand cats went to bed hungry!

The next morning the city was found to have been placarded during the night with a proclamation of the Federated Union of Old Maids. This ancient and powerful order averred through its Supreme Executive Head that the boycotting of my father and the retaliatory lock-out of my mother were seriously imperiling the interests of religion. The proclamation went on to state that if arbitration were not adopted by noon that day all the old maids of the federation would strike—and strike they did.

The next act of this unhappy drama was an insurrection of cats.

These sacred animals, seeing themselves doomed to starvation, held a mass-meeting and marched in procession through the streets, swearing and spitting like fiends. This revolt of the gods produced such consternation that many pious persons died of fright and all business was suspended to bury them and pass terrifying resolutions.

Matters were now about as bad as it seemed possible for them to be. Meetings among representatives of the hostile interests were held, but no understanding was arrived at that would hold. Every agreement was broken as soon as made, and each element of the discord was frantically appealing to the peoples. A new horror was in store.

It will be remembered that my father was a deodorizer of dead dogs, but was unable to practice his useful and humble profession because no one would employ him. The dead dogs in consequence reeked rascally. Then they struck! From every vacant lot and public dumping ground, from every hedge and ditch and gutter and cistern, every crystal rill and the clabbered waters of all the canals and estuaries—from all the places, in short, which from time immemorial have been preempted by dead dogs and consecrated to the uses of them and their heirs and successors forever—they trooped innumerous, a ghastly crew! Their procession was a mile in length. Midway of the town it met the procession of cats in full song. The cats instantly exalted their backs and magnified their tails; the dead dogs uncovered their teeth as in life, and erected such of their bristles as still adhered to the skin.

The carnage that ensued was too awful for relation! The light of the sun was obscured by flying fur, and the battle was waged in the darkness, blindly and regardless. The swearing of the cats was audible miles away, while the fragrance of the dead dogs desolated seven provinces.

How the battle might have resulted it is impossible to say, but when it was at its fiercest the Federated Union of Old Maids came running down a side street and sprang into the thickest of the fray. A moment later my mother herself bore down upon the warring hosts, brandishing a cleaver, and laid about her with great freedom and impartiality. My father joined the fight, the municipal authorities engaged, and the general public, converging on the battlefield from all points of the compass, consumed itself in the center as it pressed in from the circumference. Last of all, the dead held a meeting in the cemetery and resolving on a general strike, began to destroy vaults, tombs, monuments, headstones, willows, angels and young sheep in marble—everything they could lay their hands on. By nightfall the living and the dead were alike exterminated, and where the ancient and sacred city of Sardasa had stood nothing remained but an excavation filled with dead bodies and building materials, shreds of cat and blue patches of decayed dog. The place is now a vast pool of stagnant water in the center of a desert.

The stirring events of those few days constituted my industrial education, and so well have I improved my advantages that I am now Chief of Misrule to the Dukes of Disorder, an organization numbering thirteen million American workingmen.

OIL OF DOG

My name is Boffer Bings. I was born of honest parents in one of the humbler walks of life, my father being a manufacturer of dog-oil and my mother having a small studio in the shadow of the village church, where she disposed of unwelcome babes. In my boyhood I was trained to habits of industry; I not only assisted my father in procuring dogs for his vats, but was frequently employed by my mother to carry away the debris of her work in the studio. In performance of this duty I sometimes had need of all my natural intelligence for all the law officers of the vicinity were opposed to my mother's business. They were not elected on an opposition ticket, and the matter had never been made a political issue; it just happened so. My father's business of making dog-oil was, naturally, less unpopular, though the owners of missing dogs sometimes regarded him with suspicion, which was reflected, to some extent, upon me. My father had, as silent partners, all the physicians of the town, who seldom wrote a prescription which did not contain what they were pleased to designate as *ol. can.* It is really the most valuable medicine ever discovered. But most persons are unwilling to make personal sacrifices for the afflicted, and it was evident that many of the fattest dogs in town had been forbidden to play with me—a fact which pained my young sensibilities, and at one time came near driving me to become a pirate.

Looking back upon those days, I cannot but regret, at times, that by indirectly bringing my beloved parents to their death I was the author of misfortunes profoundly affecting my future.

One evening while passing my father's oil factory with the body of a foundling from my mother's studio I saw a constable who seemed to be closely watching my movements. Young as I was, I had learned that a constable's acts, of whatever apparent character, are prompted by the most reprehensible motives, and I avoided him by dodging into the oilery by a side door which happened to stand ajar. I locked it at once and was alone with my dead. My father had retired for the night. The only light in the place came from the furnace, which glowed a deep, rich crimson under one of the vats, casting ruddy reflections on the walls. Within the cauldron the oil still rolled in indolent ebullition, occasionally pushing to the surface a piece of dog. Seating myself to wait for the constable to go away, I held the naked body of the foundling in my lap and tenderly stroked its short silken hair. Ah, how beautiful it was! Even at that early age I was passionately fond of children, and as I looked upon this cherub I could almost find it in my heart to wish that the small, red wound upon its breast—the work of my dear mother—had not been mortal.

It had been my custom to throw the babes into the river which nature had thoughtfully provided for the purpose, but that night I did not dare to leave the oilery for fear of the constable. "After all," I said to myself, "it cannot greatly matter if I put it into this cauldron. My father will never know the bones from those of a puppy and the few deaths which may result from administering another kind of oil for the incomparable *ol. can.* are not important in a population which increases so rapidly." In short, I took the first step in crime and brought myself untold sorrow by casting the babe into the cauldron.

The next day, somewhat to my surprise, my father, rubbing his hands with satisfaction, informed me and my mother that he had obtained the finest quality of oil that was ever seen; that the physicians to whom he had shown samples had so pronounced it. He added that he had no knowledge as to how the result was obtained; the dogs had been treated in all respects as usual, and were of an ordinary breed. I deemed it my duty to explain—which I did, though palsied would have been my tongue if I could have foreseen the consequences. Bewailing their previous ignorance of the advantages of combining their industries, my parents at once took measures to repair the error. My mother removed her studio to a wing of the factory building and my duties in connection with the business ceased; I was no longer required to dispose of the bodies of the small superfluous, and there was no need of alluring dogs to their doom, for my father discarded them altogether, though they still had an honorable place in the name of the oil. So suddenly thrown into idleness, I might naturally have been expected to become vicious and dissolute, but I did not. The holy influence of my dear mother was ever about me to protect me from the temptations which beset youth, and my father was a deacon in a church. Alas, that through my fault these estimable persons should have come to so bad an end!

Finding a double profit in her business, my mother now devoted herself to it with a new assiduity. She removed not only superfluous and unwelcome babes to order, but went out into the highways and byways, gathering in children of a larger growth, and even such adults as she could entice to the oilery. My father, too, enamored of the superior quality of oil produced, purveyed for his vats with diligence and zeal. The conversion of their neighbors into dog-oil became, in short, the one passion of their lives—an absorbing and overwhelming greed took possession of their souls and served them in place of a hope in Heaven—by which, also, they were inspired.

So enterprising had they now become that a public meeting was held and resolutions passed severely censuring them. It was intimated by the chairman that any further raids upon the population would be met in a spirit of hostility. My poor parents left the meeting broken-hearted, desperate and, I believe, not altogether sane. Anyhow, I deemed it prudent not to enter the oilery with them that night, but slept outside in a stable.

At about midnight some mysterious impulse caused me to rise and peer through a window into the furnace-room, where I knew my father now slept. The fires were burning as brightly as if the following day's harvest had been expected to be abundant. One of the large cauldrons was slowly "walloping" with a mysterious appearance of self-restraint, as if it bided its time to put forth its full energy. My father was not in bed; he had risen in his nightclothes and was preparing a noose in a strong cord. From the looks which he cast at the door of my mother's bedroom I knew too well the purpose that he had in mind. Speechless and motionless with terror, I could do nothing in prevention or warning. Suddenly the door of my mother's apartment was opened, noiselessly, and the two confronted each other, both apparently surprised. The lady, also, was in her nightclothes, and she held in her right hand the tool of her trade, a long, narrow-bladed dagger.

She, too, had been unable to deny herself the last profit which the unfriendly action of the citizens and my absence had left her. For one instant they looked into each other's blazing eyes and then sprang together with indescribable fury. Round and round the room they struggled, the man cursing, the woman shrieking, both fighting like demons—she to strike him with the dagger, he to strangle her with his great bare hands. I know not how long I had the unhappiness to observe this disagreeable instance of domestic infelicity, but at last, after a more than usually vigorous struggle, the combatants suddenly moved apart.

My father's breast and my mother's weapon showed evidences of contact. For another instant they glared at each other in the most unamiable way; then my poor, wounded father, feeling the hand of death upon him, leaped forward, unmindful of resistance, grasped my dear mother in his arms, dragged her to the side of the boiling cauldron, collected all his failing energies, and sprang in with her! In a moment, both had disappeared and were adding their oil to that of the committee of citizens who had called the day before with an invitation to the public meeting.

Convinced that these unhappy events closed to me every avenue to an honorable career in that town, I removed to the famous city of Otumwee, where these memoirs are written with a heart full of remorse for a heedless act entailing so dismal a commercial disaster.

CURRIED COW

My Aunt Patience, who tilled a small farm in the state of Michigan, had a favorite cow. This creature was not a good cow, nor a profitable one, for instead of devoting a part of her leisure to secretion of milk and production of veal she concentrated all her faculties on the study of kicking. She would kick all day and get up in the middle of the night to kick. She would kick at anything—hens, pigs, posts, loose stones, birds in the air and fish leaping out of the water; to this impartial and catholic-minded beef, all were equal—all similarly undeserving. Like old Timotheus, who "raised a mortal to the skies," was my Aunt Patience's cow; though, in the words of a later poet than Dryden, she did it "more harder and more frequently." It was pleasing to see her open a passage for herself through a populous barnyard. She would flash out, right and left, first with one hind leg and then with the other, and would sometimes, under favoring conditions, have a considerable number of domestic animals in the air at once.

Her kicks, too, were as admirable in quality as inexhaustible in quantity. They were incomparably superior to those of the untutored kine that had not made the art a life study—mere amateurs that kicked "by ear," as they say in music. I saw her once standing in the road, professedly fast asleep, and mechanically munching her cud with a sort of Sunday morning lassitude, as one munches one's cud in a dream. Snouting about at her side, blissfully unconscious of impending danger and wrapped up in thoughts of his sweetheart, was a gigantic black hog—a hog of about the size and general appearance of a yearling rhinoceros. Suddenly, while I looked—without a visible movement on the part of the cow—with never a perceptible tremor of her frame, nor a lapse in the placid regularity of her chewing—that hog had gone away from there—had utterly taken his leave. But away toward the pale horizon a minute black speck was traversing the empyrean with the speed of a meteor, and in a moment had disappeared, without audible report, beyond the distant hills. It may have been that hog.

Currying cows is not, I think, a common practice, even in Michigan; but as this one had never needed milking, of course she had to be subjected to some equivalent form of persecution; and irritating her skin with a currycomb was thought as disagreeable an attention as a thoughtful affection could devise. At least she thought it so; though I suspect her mistress really meant it for the good creature's temporal advantage. Anyhow my aunt always made it a condition to the employment of a farm-servant that he should curry the cow every morning; but after just enough trials to convince himself that it was not a sudden spasm, nor a mere local disturbance, the man would always give notice of an intention to quit by pounding the beast half-dead with some foreign body and then limping home to his couch. I don't know how many men the creature removed from my aunt's employ in this way, but judging from the number of lame persons in that part of the country, I should say a good many; though some of the lameness may have been taken at second-hand from the original sufferers by their descendants, and some may have come by contagion.

I think my aunt's was a faulty system of agriculture. It is true her farm labor cost her nothing, for the laborers all left her service before any salary had accrued; but as the cow's fame spread abroad through the several States and Territories, it became increasingly difficult to obtain hands; and, after all, the favorite was imperfectly curried. It was currently remarked that the cow had kicked the farm to pieces—a rude metaphor, implying that the land was not properly cultivated, nor the buildings and fences kept in adequate repair.

It was useless to remonstrate with my aunt: she would concede everything, amending nothing. Her late husband had attempted to reform the abuse in this manner, and had had the argument all his own way until he had remonstrated himself into an early grave; and the funeral was delayed all day, until a fresh undertaker could be procured, the one originally engaged having confidingly undertaken to curry the cow at the request of the widow.

Since that time my Aunt Patience had not been in the matrimonial market; the love of that cow had usurped in her heart the place of a more natural and profitable affection. But when she saw her seeds unsown, her harvests ungarnered, her fences overtopped with rank brambles and her meadows gorgeous with the towering Canada thistle she thought it best to take a partner.

When it transpired that my Aunt Patience intended wedlock there was intense popular excitement. Every adult single male became at once a marrying man. The criminal statistics of Badger County show that in that single year more marriages occurred than in any decade before or since. But none of them was my aunt's. Men married their cooks, their laundresses, their deceased wives' mothers, their enemies' sisters—married whomsoever would wed; and any man who, by fair means or courtship, could not obtain a wife went before a justice of the peace and made an affidavit that he had some wives in Indiana. Such was the fear of being married alive by my Aunt Patience.

Now, where my aunt's affection was concerned she was, as the reader will have already surmised, a rather determined woman; and the extraordinary marrying epidemic having left but one eligible male in all that county, she had set her heart upon that one eligible male; then she went and carted him to her home. He turned out to be a long Methodist parson, named Huggins.

Aside from his unconscionable length, the Rev. Berosus Huggins was not so bad a fellow, and was nobody's fool. He was, I suppose, the most ill-favored mortal, however, in the whole northern half of America—thin, angular, cadaverous of visage and solemn out of all reason. He commonly wore a low-crowned black hat, set so far down upon his head as partly to eclipse his eyes and wholly obscure the ample glory of his ears. The only other visible article of his attire (except a brace of wrinkled cowskin boots, by which the word "polish" would have been considered the meaningless fragment of a lost language) was a tight-fitting black frock-coat, preternaturally long in the waist, the skirts of which fell about his heels, sopping up the dew. This he always wore snugly buttoned from the throat downward. In this attire he cut a tolerably spectral figure. His aspect was so conspicuously unnatural and inhuman that whenever he went into a cornfield, the predatory crows would temporarily forsake their business to settle upon him in swarms, fighting for the best seats upon his person, by way of testifying their contempt for the weak inventions of the husbandman.

The day after the wedding my Aunt Patience summoned the Rev. Berosus to the council chamber, and uttered her mind to the following intent:

"Now, Huggy, dear, I'll tell you what there is to do about the place. First, you must repair all the fences, clearing out the weeds and repressing the brambles with a strong hand. Then you will have to exterminate the Canadian thistles, mend the wagon, rig up a plow or two, and get things into ship-shape generally. This will keep you out of mischief for the better part of two years; of course you will have to give up preaching, for the present. As soon as you have—O! I forgot poor Phœbe. She"—

"Mrs. Huggins," interrupted her solemn spouse, "I shall hope to be the means, under Providence, of effecting all needful reforms in the husbandry of this farm. But the sister you mention (I trust she is not of the world's people)—have I the pleasure of knowing her? The name, indeed, sounds familiar, but"—

"Not know Phœbe!" cried my aunt, with unfeigned astonishment; "I thought everybody in Badger knew Phœbe. Why, you will have to scratch her legs, every blessed morning of your natural life!"

"I assure you, madam," rejoined the Rev. Berosus, with dignity, "it would yield me a hallowed pleasure to minister to the spiritual needs of sister Phœbe, to the extent of my feeble and unworthy ability; but, really, I fear the merely secular ministration of which you speak must be entrusted to abler and, I would respectfully suggest, female hands.

"Whyyy, youuu ooold, foooool!" replied my aunt, spreading her eyes with unbounded amazement, "Phœbe is a cow!"

"In that case," said the husband, with unruffled composure, "it will, of course, devolve upon me to see that her carnal welfare is properly attended to; and I shall be happy to bestow upon her legs such time as I may, without sin, snatch from my strife with Satan and the Canadian thistles."

With that the Rev. Mr. Huggins crowded his hat upon his shoulders, pronounced a brief benediction upon his bride, and betook himself to the barn-yard.

Now, it is necessary to explain that he had known from the first who Phœbe was, and was familiar, from hearsay, with all her sinful traits. Moreover, he had already done himself the honor of making her a visit, remaining in the vicinity of her person, just out of range, for more than an hour and permitting her to survey him at her leisure from every point of the compass. In short, he and Phœbe had mutually reconnoitered and prepared for action.

Amongst the articles of comfort and luxury which went to make up the good parson's *dot,* and which his wife had already caused to be conveyed to his new home, was a patent cast-iron pump, about seven feet high. This had been deposited near the barn-yard, preparatory to being set up on the planks above the barn-yard well. Mr. Huggins now sought out this invention and conveying it to its destination put it into position, screwing it firmly to the planks. He next divested himself of his long gaberdine and his hat, buttoning the former loosely about the pump, which it almost concealed, and hanging the latter upon the summit of the structure. The handle of the pump, when depressed, curved outwardly between the coat-skirts, singularly like a tail, but with this inconspicuous exception, any unprejudiced observer would have pronounced the thing Mr. Huggins, looking uncommonly well.

The preliminaries completed, the good man carefully closed the gate of the barnyard, knowing that as soon as Phœbe, who was campaigning in the kitchen garden, should note the precaution she would come and jump in to frustrate it, which eventually she did. Her master, meanwhile, had laid himself, coatless and hatless, along the outside of the close board fence, where he put in the time pleasantly, catching his death of cold and peering through a knot-hole.

At first, and for some time, the animal pretended not to see the figure on the platform. Indeed she had turned her back upon it directly she arrived, affecting a light sleep. Finding that this stratagem did not achieve the success that she had expected, she abandoned it and stood for several minutes irresolute, munching her cud in a half-hearted way, but obviously thinking very hard. Then she began nosing along the ground as if wholly absorbed in a search for something that she had lost, tacking about hither and thither, but all the time drawing nearer to the object of her wicked intention. Arrived within speaking distance, she stood for a little while confronting the fraud-ful figure, then put out her nose toward it, as if to be caressed, trying to create the impression that fondling and dalliance were more to her than wealth, power and the plaudits of the populace—that she had been accustomed to them all her sweet young life and could not get on without them. Then she approached a little nearer, as if to shake hands, all the while maintaining the most amiable expression of countenance and executing all manner of seductive nods and winks and smiles. Suddenly she wheeled about and with the rapidity of lightning dealt out a terrible kick—a kick of inconceivable force and fury, comparable to nothing in nature but a stroke of paralysis out of a clear sky!

The effect was magical! Cows kick, not backward but sidewise. The impact which was intended to project the counterfeit theologian into the middle of the succeeding conference week reacted upon the animal herself, and it and the pain together set her spinning like a top. Such was the velocity of her revolution that she looked like a dim, circular cow, surrounded by a continuous ring like that of the planet Saturn—the white tuft at the extremity of her sweeping tail! Presently, as the sustaining centrifugal force lessened and failed, she began to sway and wabble from side to side, and finally, toppling over on her side, rolled convulsively on her back and lay motionless with all her feet in the air, honestly believing that the world had somehow got atop of her and she was supporting it at a great sacrifice of personal comfort. Then she fainted.

How long she lay unconscious she knew not, but at last she unclosed her eyes, and catching sight of the open door of her stall, "more sweet than all the landscape smiling near," she struggled up, stood wavering upon three legs, rubbed her eyes, and was visibly bewildered as to the points of the compass. Observing the iron clergyman standing fast by its faith, she threw it a look of grieved reproach and hobbled heart-broken into her humble habitation, a subjugated cow.

For several weeks Phœbe's right hind leg was swollen to a monstrous growth, but by a season of judicious nursing she was "brought round all right," as her sympathetic and puzzled mistress phrased it, or "made whole," as the reticent man of God preferred to say. She was now as tractable and inoffensive "in her daily walk and conversation" (Huggins) as a little child. Her new master used to take her ailing leg trustfully into his lap, and for that matter, might have taken it into his mouth if he had so desired. Her entire character appeared to be radically changed—so altered that one day my Aunt Patience, who, fondly as she loved her, had never before so much as ventured to touch the hem of her garment, as it were, went confidently up to her to soothe her with a pan of turnips. Gad! how thinly she spread out that good old lady upon the face of an adjacent stone wall! You could not have done it so evenly with a trowel.

HAÏTA THE SHEPHERD

In the heart of Haïta the illusions of youth had not been supplanted by those of age and experience. His thoughts were pure and pleasant, for his life was simple and his soul devoid of ambition. He rose with the sun and went forth to pray at the shrine of Hastur, the god of shepherds, who heard and was pleased. After performance of this pious rite Haïta unbarred the gate of the fold and with a cheerful mind drove his flock afield, eating his morning meal of curds and oat cake as he went, occasionally pausing to add a few berries, cold with dew, or to drink of the waters that came away from the hills to join the stream in the middle of the valley and be borne along with it, he knew not whither.

During the long summer day, as his sheep cropped the good grass which the gods had made to grow for them, or lay with their forelegs doubled under their breasts and chewed the cud, Haïta, reclining in the shadow of a tree, or sitting upon a rock, played so sweet music upon his reed pipe that sometimes from the corner of his eye he got accidental glimpses of the minor sylvan deities, leaning forward out of the copse to hear; but if he looked at them directly they vanished. From this—for he must be thinking if he would not turn into one of his own sheep—he drew the solemn inference that happiness may come if not sought, but if looked for will never be seen; for next to the favor of Hastur, who never disclosed himself, Haïta most valued the friendly interest of his neighbors, the shy immortals of the wood and stream. At nightfall he drove his flock back to the fold, saw that the gate was secure and retired to his cave for refreshment and for dreams.

So passed his life, one day like another, save when the storms uttered the wrath of an offended god. Then Haïta cowered in his cave, his face hidden in his hands, and prayed that he alone might be punished for his sins and the world saved from destruction. Sometimes when there was a great rain, and the stream came out of its banks, compelling him to urge his terrified flock to the uplands, he interceded for the people in the cities which he had been told lay in the plain beyond the two blue hills forming the gateway of his valley.

"It is kind of thee, O Hastur," so he prayed, "to give me mountains so near to my dwelling and my fold that I and my sheep can escape the angry torrents; but the rest of the world thou must thyself deliver in some way that I know not of, or I will no longer worship thee."

And Hastur, knowing that Haïta was a youth who kept his word, spared the cities and turned the waters into the sea.

So he had lived since he could remember. He could not rightly conceive any other mode of existence. The holy hermit who dwelt at the head of the valley, a full hour's journey away, from whom he had heard the tale of the great cities where dwelt people—poor souls!—who had no sheep, gave him no knowledge of that early time, when, so he reasoned, he must have been small and helpless like a lamb.

It was through thinking on these mysteries and marvels, and on that horrible change to silence and decay which he felt sure must some time come to him, as he had seen it come to so many of his flock—as it came to all living things except the birds—that Haïta first became conscious how miserable and hopeless was his lot.

"It is necessary," he said, "that I know whence and how I came; for how can one perform his duties unless able to judge what they are by the way in which he was intrusted with them? And what contentment can I have when I know not how long it is going to last? Perhaps before another sun I may be changed, and then what will become of the sheep? What, indeed, will have become of me?"

Pondering these things Haïta became melancholy and morose. He no longer spoke cheerfully to his flock, nor ran with alacrity to the shrine of Hastur. In every breeze he heard whispers of malign deities whose existence he now first observed. Every cloud was a portent signifying disaster, and the darkness was full of terrors. His reed pipe when applied to his lips gave out no melody, but a dismal wail; the sylvan and riparian intelligences no longer thronged the thicketside to listen, but fled from the sound, as he knew by the stirred leaves and bent flowers. He relaxed his vigilance and many of his sheep strayed away into the hills and were lost. Those that remained became lean and ill for lack of good pasturage, for he would not seek it for them, but conducted them day after day to the same spot, through mere abstraction, while puzzling about life and death—of immortality he knew not.

One day while indulging in the gloomiest reflections he suddenly sprang from the rock upon which he sat, and with a determined gesture of the right hand exclaimed: "I will no longer be a suppliant for knowledge which the gods withhold. Let them look to it that they do me no wrong. I will do my duty as best I can and if I err upon their own heads be it!"

Suddenly, as he spoke, a great brightness fell about him, causing him to look upward, thinking the sun had burst through a rift in the clouds; but there were no clouds. No more than an arm's length away stood a beautiful maiden. So beautiful she was that the flowers about her feet folded their petals in despair and bent their heads in token of submission; so sweet her look that the humming birds thronged her eyes, thrusting their thirsty bills almost into them, and the wild bees were about her lips. And such was her brightness that the shadows of all objects lay divergent from her feet, turning as she moved.

Haïta was entranced. Rising, he knelt before her in adoration, and she laid her hand upon his head.

"Come," she said in a voice that had the music of all the bells of his flock—"come, thou art not to worship me, who am no goddess, but if thou art truthful and dutiful I will abide with thee."

Haïta seized her hand, and stammering his joy and gratitude arose, and hand in hand they stood and smiled into each other's eyes. He gazed on her with reverence and rapture. He said: "I pray thee, lovely maid, tell me thy name and whence and why thou comest."

At this she laid a warning finger on her lip and began to withdraw. Her beauty underwent a visible alteration that made him shudder, he knew not why, for still she was beautiful. The landscape was darkened by a giant shadow sweeping across the valley with the speed of a vulture. In the obscurity the maiden's figure grew dim and indistinct and her voice seemed to come from a distance, as she said, in a tone of sorrowful reproach: "Presumptuous and ungrateful youth! must I then so soon leave thee? Would nothing do but thou must at once break the eternal compact?"

Inexpressibly grieved, Haïta fell upon his knees and implored her to remain—rose and sought her in the deepening darkness—ran in circles, calling to her aloud, but all in vain. She was no longer visible, but out of the gloom he heard her voice saying:

"Nay, thou shalt not have me by seeking. Go to thy duty, faithless shepherd, or we shall never meet again."

Night had fallen; the wolves were howling in the hills and the terrified sheep crowding about Haïta's feet. In the demands of the hour he forgot his disappointment, drove his sheep to the fold and repairing to the place of worship poured out his heart in gratitude to Hastur for permitting him to save his flock, then retired to his cave and slept.

When Haïta awoke the sun was high and shone in at the cave, illuminating it with a great glory. And there, beside him, sat the maiden. She smiled upon him with a smile that seemed the visible music of his pipe of reeds. He dared not speak, fearing to offend her as before, for he knew not what he could venture to say.

"Because," she said, "thou didst thy duty by the flock, and didst not forget to thank Hastur for staying the wolves of the night, I am come to thee again. Wilt thou have me for a companion?"

"Who would not have thee forever?" replied Haïta. "Oh! never again leave me until—until I—change and become silent and motionless."

Haïta had no word for death.

"I wish, indeed," he continued, "that thou wert of my own sex, that we might wrestle and run races and so never tire of being together."

At these words the maiden arose and passed out of the cave, and Haïta, springing from his couch of fragrant boughs to overtake and detain her, observed to his astonishment that the rain was falling and the stream in the middle of the valley had come out of its banks. The sheep were bleating in terror, for the rising waters had invaded their fold. And there was danger for the unknown cities of the distant plain.

It was many days before Haïta saw the maiden again. One day he was returning from the head of the valley, where he had gone with ewe's milk and oat cake and berries for the holy hermit, who was too old and feeble to provide himself with food.

"Poor old man!" he said aloud, as he trudged along homeward. "I will return to-morrow and bear him on my back to my own dwelling, where I can care for him. Doubtless it is for this that Hastur has reared me all these many years, and gives me health and strength."

As he spoke, the maiden, clad in glittering garments, met him in the path with a smile that took away his breath.

"I am come again," she said, "to dwell with thee if thou wilt now have me, for none else will. Thou mayest have learned wisdom, and art willing to take me as I am, nor care to know."

Haïta threw himself at her feet. "Beautiful being," he cried, "if thou wilt but deign to accept all the devotion of my heart and soul—after Hastur be served—it is thine forever. But, alas! thou art capricious and wayward. Before to-morrow's sun I may lose thee again. Promise, I beseech thee, that however in my ignorance I may offend, thou wilt forgive and remain always with me."

Scarcely had he finished speaking when a troop of bears came out of the hills, racing toward him with crimson mouths and fiery eyes. The maiden again vanished, and he turned and fled for his life. Nor did he stop until he was in the cot of the holy hermit, whence he had set out. Hastily barring the door against the bears he cast himself upon the ground and wept.

"My son," said the hermit from his couch of straw, freshly gathered that morning by Haïta's hands, "it is not like thee to weep for bears—tell me what sorrow hath befallen thee, that age may minister to the hurts of youth with such balms as it hath of its wisdom."

Haïta told him all: how thrice he had met the radiant maid, and thrice she had left him forlorn. He related minutely all that had passed between them, omitting no word of what had been said.

When he had ended, the holy hermit was a moment silent, then said: "My son, I have attended to thy story, and I know the maiden. I have myself seen her, as have many. Know, then, that her name, which she would not even permit thee to inquire, is Happiness. Thou saidst the truth to her, that she is capricious for she imposeth conditions that man can not fulfill, and delinquency is punished by desertion. She cometh only when unsought, and will not be questioned. One manifestation of curiosity, one sign of doubt, one expression of misgiving, and she is away! How long didst thou have her at any time before she fled?"

"Only a single instant," answered Haïta, blushing with shame at the confession. "Each time I drove her away in one moment."

"Unfortunate youth!" said the holy hermit, "but for thine indiscretion thou mightst have had her for two."

AN IMPERFECT CONFLAGRATION

Early one June morning in 1872 I murdered my father—an act which made a deep impression on me at the time. This was before my marriage, while I was living with my parents in Wisconsin. My father and I were in the library of our home, dividing the proceeds of a burglary which we had committed that night. These consisted of household goods mostly, and the task of equitable division was difficult. We got on very well with the napkins, towels and such things, and the silverware was parted pretty nearly equally, but you can see for yourself that when you try to divide a single music-box by two without a remainder you will have trouble. It was that music box which brought disaster and disgrace upon our family. If we had left it my poor father might now be alive.

It was a most exquisite and beautiful piece of workmanship—inlaid with costly woods and carven very curiously. It would not only play a great variety of tunes, but would whistle like a quail, bark like a dog, crow every morning at daylight whether it was wound up or not, and break the Ten Commandments. It was this last mentioned accomplishment that won my father's heart and caused him to commit the only dishonorable act of his life, though possibly he would have committed more if he had been spared: he tried to conceal that music-box from me, and declared upon his honor that he had not taken it, though I knew very well that, so far as he was concerned, the burglary had been undertaken chiefly for the purpose of obtaining it.

My father had the music-box hidden under his cloak; we had worn cloaks by way of disguise. He had solemnly assured me that he did not take it. I knew that he did, and knew something of which he was evidently ignorant; namely, that the box would crow at daylight and betray him if I could prolong the division of profits till that time. All occurred as I wished: as the gaslight began to pale in the library and the shape of the windows was seen dimly behind the curtains, a long cock-a-doodle-doo came from beneath the old gentle-man's cloak, followed by a few bars of an aria from *Tannhauser,* ending with a loud click. A small hand-axe, which we had used to break into the unlucky house, lay between us on the table; I picked it up. The old man seeing that further concealment was useless took the box from under his cloak and set it on the table. "Cut it in two if you prefer that plan," said he; "I tried to save it from destruction."

He was a passionate lover of music and could himself play the concertina with expression and feeling.

I said: "I do not question the purity of your

motive: it would be presumptuous in me to sit in judgment on my father. But business is business, and with this axe I am going to effect a dissolution of our partnership unless you will consent in all future burglaries to wear a bell-punch."

"No," he said, after some reflection, "no, I could not do that; it would look like a confession of dishonesty. People would say that you distrusted me."

I could not help admiring his spirit and sensitiveness; for a moment I was proud of him and disposed to overlook his fault, but a glance at the richly jeweled music-box decided me, and, as I said, I removed the old man from this vale of tears. Having done so, I was a trifle uneasy. Not only was he my father—the author of my being—but the body would be certainly discovered. It was now broad daylight and my mother was likely to enter the library at any moment. Under the circumstances, I thought it expedient to remove her also, which I did. Then I paid off all the servants and discharged them.

That afternoon I went to the chief of police, told him what I had done and asked his advice. It would be very painful to me if the facts became publicly known. My conduct would be generally condemned; the newspapers would bring it up against me if ever I should run for office. The chief saw the force of these considerations; he was himself an assassin of wide experience. After consulting with the presiding judge of the Court of Variable Jurisdiction he advised me to conceal the bodies in one of the book-cases, get a heavy insurance on the house and burn it down. This I proceeded to do.

In the library was a book-case which my father had recently purchased of some cranky inventor and had not filled. It was in shape and size something like the old-fashioned "wardrobes" which one sees in bed-rooms without closets, but opened all the way down, like a woman's night-dress. It had glass doors. I had recently laid out my parents and they were now rigid enough to stand erect; so I stood them in this book-case, from which I had removed the shelves. I locked them in and tacked some curtains over the glass doors. The inspector from the insurance office passed a half-dozen times before the case without suspicion.

That night, after getting my policy, I set fire to the house and started through the woods to town, two miles away, where I managed to be found about the time the excitement was at its height. With cries of apprehension for the fate of my parents, I joined the rush and arrived at the fire some two hours after I had kindled it. The whole town was there as I dashed up. The house was entirely consumed, but in one end of the level bed of glowing embers, bolt upright and uninjured, was that book-case! The curtains had burned away, exposing the glass doors, through which the fierce, red light illuminated the interior. There stood my dear father "in his habit as he lived," and at his side the partner of his joys and sorrows. Not a hair of them was singed, their clothing was intact. On their heads and throats the injuries which in the accomplishment of my designs I had been compelled to inflict were conspicuous. As in the presence of a miracle, the people were silent; awe and terror had stilled every tongue. I was myself greatly affected.

Some three years later, when the events herein related had nearly faded from my memory, I went to New York to assist in passing some counterfeit United States bonds. Carelessly looking into a furniture store one day, I saw the exact counterpart of that book-case. "I bought it for a trifle from a reformed inventor," the dealer explained. "He said it was fireproof, the pores of the wood being filled with alum under hydraulic pressure and the glass made of asbestos. I don't suppose it is really fireproof—you can have it at the price of an ordinary book-case."

"No," I said, "if you cannot warrant it fireproof I won't take it"—and I bade him good morning.

I would not have had it at any price: it revived memories that were exceedingly disagreeable.

THE WIDOWER TURMORE

The circumstances under which Joram Turmore became a widower have never been popularly understood. I know them, naturally, for I am Joram Turmore; and my wife, the late Elizabeth Mary Turmore, is by no means ignorant of them; but although she doubtless relates them, yet they remain a secret, for not a soul has ever believed her.

When I married Elizabeth Mary Johnin she was very wealthy, otherwise I could hardly have afforded to marry, for I had not a cent, and Heaven had not put into my heart any intention to earn one. I held the Professorship of Cats in the University of Graymaulkin, and scholastic pursuits had unfitted me for the heat and burden of business or labor. Moreover, I could not forget that I was a Turmore—a member of a family whose motto from the time of William of Normandy has been *Laborare est errare.* The only known infracton of the sacred family tradition occurred when Sir Aldebaran Turmore de Peters-Turmore, an illustrious master burglar of the seventeenth century, personally assisted at a difficult operation undertaken by some of his workmen. That blot upon our escutcheon cannot be contemplated without the most poignant mortification.

My incumbency of the Chair of Cats in the Graymaulkin University had not, of course, been marked by any instance of mean industry. There had never, at any one time, been more than two students of the Noble Science, and by merely repeating the manuscript lectures of my predecessor, which I had found among his effects (he died at sea on his way to Malta) I could sufficiently sate their famine for knowledge without really earning even the distinction which served in place of salary.

Naturally, under the straitened circumstances, I regarded Elizabeth Mary as a kind of special Providence. She unwisely refused to share her fortune with me, but for that I cared nothing; for, although by the laws of that country (as is well known) a wife has control of her separate property during her life, it passes to the husband at her death; nor can she dispose of it otherwise by will. The mortality among wives is considerable, but not excessive.

Having married Elizabeth Mary and, as it were, ennobled her by making her a Turmore, I felt that the manner of her death ought, in some sense, to match her social distinction. If I should remove her by any of the ordinary marital methods I should incur a just reproach, as one destitute of a proper family pride. Yet I could not hit upon a suitable plan.

In this emergency I decided to consult the Turmore archives, a priceless collection of documents, comprising the records of the family from the time of its founder in the seventh century of our era. I knew that among these sacred muniments I should find detailed accounts of all the principal murders committed by my sainted ancestors for forty generations. From that mass of papers I could hardly fail to derive the most valuable suggestions

The collection contained also most interesting relics. There were patents of nobility granted to my forefathers for daring and ingenious removals of pretenders to thrones, or occupants of them; stars, crosses and other decorations attesting services of the most secret and unmentionable character; miscellaneous gifts from the world's greatest conspirators representing an intrinsic money value beyond computation. There were robes, jewels, swords of honor, and every kind of "testimonials of esteem"; a king's skull fashioned into a wine cup; the title deeds to vast estates, long alienated by confiscation, sale, or abandonment; an illuminated breviary that had belonged to Sir Aldebaran Turmore de Peters-Turmore of accursed memory; embalmed ears of several of the family's most renowned enemies; the small intestine of a certain unworthy Italian statesman inimical to Turmores, which, twisted into a jumping rope, had served the youth of six kindred generations—mementoes and souvenirs precious beyond the appraisals of imagination, but by the sacred mandates of tradition and sentiment forever inalienable by sale or gift.

As the head of the family, I was custodian of all these priceless heirlooms, and for their safe keeping had constructed in the basement of my dwelling a strong-room of massive masonry, whose solid stone walls and single iron door could defy alike the earthquake's shock, the tireless assaults of Time, and Cupidity's unholy hand.

To this thesaurus of the soul, redolent of sentiment and tenderness, and rich in suggestions of crime, I now repaired for hints upon assassination. To my unspeakable astonishment and grief I found it empty! Every shelf, every chest, every coffer had been rifled. Of that unique and incomparable collection not a vestige remained! Yet I proved that until I had myself unlocked the massive metal door, not a bolt nor bar had been disturbed; the seals upon the lock had been intact.

I passed the night in alternate lamentation and research, equally fruitless; the mystery was impenetrable to conjecture, the pain invincible to balm. But never once throughout that dreadful night did my firm spirit relinquish its high design against Elizabeth Mary, and daybreak found me more resolute than before to harvest the fruits of my marriage. My great loss seemed but to bring me into nearer spiritual relations with my dead ancestors, and to lay upon me a new and more inevitable obedience to the suasion that spoke in every globule of my blood.

My plan of action was soon formed, and procuring a stout cord I entered my wife's bedroom, finding her, as I expected, in a sound sleep. Before she was awake, I had her bound fast, hand and foot.

She was greatly surprised and pained, but heedless of her remonstrances, delivered in a high key, I carried her into the now rifled strong-room, which I had never suffered her to enter, and of whose treasures I had not apprised her. Seating her, still bound, in an angle of the wall, I passed the next two days and nights in conveying bricks and mortar to the spot, and on the morning of the third day had her securely walled in, from floor to ceiling. All this time I gave no further heed to her pleas for mercy than (on her assurance of non-resistance, which I am bound to say she honorably observed) to grant her the freedom of her limbs. The space allowed her was about four feet by six. As I inserted the last bricks of the top course, in contact with the ceiling of the strong-room, she bade me farewell with what I deemed the composure of despair, and I rested from my work, feeling that I had faithfully observed the traditions of an ancient and illustrious family. My only bitter reflection, so far as my own conduct was concerned, came of the consciousness that in the performance of my design I had labored; but this no living soul would ever know.

After a night's rest I went to the Judge of the Court of Successions and Inheritances and made a true and sworn relation of all that I had done—except that I ascribed to a servant the manual labor of building the wall. His honor appointed a court commissioner, who made a careful examination of the work, and upon his report Elizabeth Mary Turmore was, at the end of a week, formally pronounced dead. By due process of law I was put into possession of her estate, and although this was not by hundreds of thousands of dollars as valuable as my lost treasures, it raised me from poverty to affluence and brought me the respect of the great and good.

Some six months after these events strange rumors reached me that the ghost of my deceased wife had been seen in several places about the country, but always at a considerable distance from Graymaulkin. These rumors, which I was unable to trace to any authentic source, differed widely in many particulars, but were alike in ascribing to the apparition a certain high degree of apparent worldly prosperity combined with an audacity most uncommon in ghosts. Not only was the spirit attired in most costly raiment, but it walked at noonday, and even drove! I was inexpressibly annoyed by these reports, and thinking there might be something more than superstition in the popular belief that only the spirits of the unburied dead still walk the earth, I took some workmen equipped with picks and crowbars into the now long unentered strong-room, and ordered them to demolish the brick wall that I had built about the partner of my joys. I was resolved to give the body of Elizabeth Mary such burial as I thought her immortal part might be willing to accept as an equivalent to the privilege of ranging at will among the haunts of the living.

In a few minutes we had broken down the wall

and, thrusting a lamp through the breach, I looked in. Nothing! Not a bone, not a lock of hair, not a shred of clothing—the narrow space which, upon my affidavit, had been legally declared to hold all that was mortal of the late Mrs. Turmore was absolutely empty! This amazing disclosure, coming upon a mind already overwrought with too much of mystery and excitement, was more than I could bear. I shrieked aloud and fell in a fit. For months afterward I lay between life and death, fevered and delirious; nor did I recover until my physician had had the providence to take a case of valuable jewels from my safe and leave the country.

The next summer I had occasion to visit my wine cellar, in one corner of which I had built the now long disused strong-room. In moving a cask of Madeira I struck it with considerable force against the partition wall, and was surprised to observe that it displaced two large square stones forming a part of the wall.

Applying my hands to these, I easily pushed them out entirely, and looking through saw that they had fallen into the niche in which I had immured my lamented wife; facing the opening which their fall left, and at a distance of four feet, was the brick-work which my own hands had made for that unfortunate gentle-woman's restraint. At this significant revelation I began a search of the wine cellar. Behind a row of casks I found four historically interesting but intrinsically valueless objects:

First, the mildewed remains of a ducal robe of state (Florentine) of the eleventh century; second, an illuminated vellum breviary with the name of Sir Aldebaran Turmore de Peters-Turmore inscribed in colors on the title page; third, a human skull fashioned into a drinking cup and deeply stained with wine; fourth, the iron cross of a Knight Commander of the Imperial Austrian Order of Assassins by Poison.

That was all—not an object having commercial value, no papers—nothing. But this was enough to clear up the mystery of the strong-room. My wife had early divined the existence and purpose of that apartment, and with the skill amounting to genius had effected an entrance by loosening the two stones in the wall.

Through that opening she had at several times abstracted the entire collection, which doubtless she had succeeded in converting into coin of the realm. When with an unconscious justice which deprives me of all satisfaction in the memory I decided to build her into the wall, by some malign fatality I selected that part of it in which were these movable stones, and doubtless before I had fairly finished my bricklaying she had removed them and, slipping through into the wine cellar, replaced them as they were originally laid. From the cellar she had easily escaped unobserved, to enjoy her infamous gains in distant parts. I have endeavored to procure a warrant, but the Lord High Baron of the Court of In-

dictment and Conviction reminds me that she is legally dead, and says my only course is to go before
the Master in Cadavery and move for a writ of dis-
interment and constructive revival. So it looks as if
I must suffer without redress this great wrong at the
hands of a woman devoid alike of principle and
shame.

A BOTTOMLESS GRAVE

My name is John Brenwalter. My father, a drunkard, had a patent for an invention for making coffee-berries out of clay; but he was an honest man and would not himself engage in the manufacture. He was, therefore, only moderately wealthy, his royalties from his really valuable invention bringing him hardly enough to pay his expenses of litigation with rogues guilty of infringement. So I lacked many advantages enjoyed by the children of unscrupulous and dishonorable parents, and had it not been for a noble and devoted mother, who neglected all my brothers and sisters and personally supervised my education, should have grown up in ignorance and been compelled to teach school. To be the favorite child of a good woman is better than gold.

When I was nineteen years of age my father had the misfortune to die. He had always had perfect health, and his death, which occurred at the dinner table without a moment's warning, surprised no one more than himself. He had that very morning been notified that a patent had been granted him for a device to burst open safes by hydraulic pressure, without noise. The Commissioner of Patents had pronounced it the most ingenious, effective and generally meritorious invention that had ever been submitted to him, and my father had naturally looked forward to an old age of prosperity and honor. His sudden death was, therefore, a deep disappointment to him; but my mother, whose piety and resignation to the will of Heaven were conspicuous virtues of her character, was apparently less affected. At the close of the meal, when my poor father's body had been removed from the floor, she called us all into an adjoining room and addressed us as follows:

"My children, the uncommon occurrence that you have just witnessed is one of the most disagreeable incidents in a good man's life, and one in which I take little pleasure, I assure you. I beg you to believe that I had no hand in bringing it about. Of course," she added, after a pause, during which her eyes were cast down in deep thought, "of course it is better that he is dead."

She uttered this with so evident a sense of its obviousness as a self-evident truth that none of us had the courage to brave her surprise by asking an explanation. My mother's air of surprise when any of us went wrong in any way was very terrible to us. One day, when in a fit of peevish temper, I had taken the liberty to cut off the baby's ear, her simple words, "John, you surprise me!" appeared to me so sharp a reproof that after a sleepless night I went to her in tears, and throwing myself at her feet, exclaimed: "Mother, forgive me for surprising you." So now we all—including the one-eared baby—felt that it would keep matters smoother to accept without question the statement that it was better, somehow, for our dear father to be dead. My mother continued:

"I must tell you, my children, that in a case of sudden and mysterious death the law requires the Coroner to come and cut the body into pieces and submit them to a number of men who, having inspected them, pronounce the person dead. For this the Coroner gets a large sum of money. I wish to avoid that painful formality in this instance; it is one which never had the approval of—of the remains. John"—here my mother turned her angel face to me—"you are an educated lad, and very discreet. You have now an opportunity to show your gratitude for all the sacrifices that your education has entailed upon the rest of us. John, go and remove the Coroner."

Inexpressibly delighted by this proof of my mother's confidence, and by the chance to distinguish myself by an act that squared with my natural disposition, I knelt before her, carried her hand to my lips and bathed it with tears of sensibility. Before five o'clock that afternoon I had removed the Coroner.

I was immediately arrested and thrown into jail, where I passed a most uncomfortable night, being unable to sleep because of the profanity of my fellow-prisoners, two clergymen, whose theological training had given them a fertility of impious ideas and a command of blasphemous language altogether unparalleled. But along toward morning the jailer, who, sleeping in an adjoining room, had been equally disturbed, entered the cell and with a fearful oath warned the reverend gentlemen that if he heard any more swearing their sacred calling would not prevent him from turning them into the street. After that they moderated their objectionable conversation, substituting an accordion, and I slept the peaceful and refreshing sleep of youth and innocence.

The next morning I was taken before the Superior Judge, sitting as a committing magistrate, and put upon my preliminary examination. I pleaded not guilty, adding that the man whom I had murdered was a notorious Democrat. (My good mother was a Republican, and from early childhood I had been carefully instructed by her in the principles of honest government and the necessity of suppressing factional opposition.) The Judge, elected by a Republican ballot-box with a sliding bottom, was visibly impressed by the cogency of my plea and offered me a cigarette.

"May it please your Honor," began the District Attorney, "I do not deem it necessary to submit any evidence in this case. Under the law of the land you sit here as a committing magistrate. It is therefore your duty to commit. Testimony and argument alike would imply a doubt that your Honor means to perform your sworn duty. That is my case."

My counsel, a brother of the deceased Coroner, rose and said: "May it please the Court, my learned friend on the other side has so well and eloquently stated the law governing in this case that it only remains for me to inquire to what extent it has been already complied with. It is true, your Honor is a committing magistrate, and as such it is your duty to commit—what? That is a matter which the law has wisely and justly left to your own discretion, and wisely you have discharged already every obligation that the law imposes. Since I have known your Honor you have done nothing but commit. You have committed embracery, theft, arson, perjury, adultery, murder—every crime in the calendar and every excess known to the sensual and depraved, including my learned friend, the District Attorney. You have done your whole duty as a committing magistrate, and as there is no evidence against this worthy young man, my client, I move that he be discharged."

An impressive silence ensued. The Judge arose, put on the black cap and in a voice trembling with emotion sentenced me to life and liberty. Then turning to my counsel he said, coldly but significantly:

"I will see you later."

The next morning the lawyer who had so conscientiously defended me against a charge of murdering his own brother—with whom he had a quarrel about some land—had disappeared and his fate is to this day unknown.

In the meantime my poor father's body had been secretly buried at midnight in the back yard of his late residence, with his late boots on and the contents of his late stomach unanalyzed. "He was opposed to display," said my dear mother, as she finished tamping down the earth above him and assisted the children to litter the place with straw; "his instincts were all domestic and he loved a quiet life."

My mother's application for letters of administration stated that she had good reason to believe that the deceased was dead, for he had not come home to his meals for several days; but the Judge of the Crowbait Court—as she ever afterward contemptuously called it—decided that the proof of death was insufficient, and put the estate into the hands of the Public Administrator, who was his son-in-law. It was found that the liabilities were exactly balanced by the assets; there was left only the patent for the device for bursting open safes without noise, by hydraulic pressure and this had passed into the ownership of the Probate Judge and the Public Administraitor—as my dear mother preferred to spell it. Thus, within a few brief months a worthy and respectable family was reduced from prosperity to crime; necessity compelled us to go to work.

In the selection of occupations we were governed by a variety of considerations, such as personal fitness, inclination, and so forth. My mother opened a select private school for instruction in the art of changing the spots upon leopard-skin rugs;

my eldest brother, George Henry, who had a turn for music, became a bugler in a neighboring asylum for deaf mutes; my sister, Mary Maria, took orders for Professor Pumpernickel's Essence of Latchkeys for flavoring mineral springs, and I set up as an adjuster and gilder of crossbeams for gibbets. The other children, too young for labor, continued to steal small articles exposed in front of shops, as they had been taught.

In our intervals of leisure we decoyed travelers into our house and buried the bodies in a cellar.

In one part of this cellar we kept wines, liquors and provisions. From the rapidity of their disappearance we acquired the superstitious belief that the spirits of the persons buried there came at dead of night and held a festival. It was at least certain that frequently of a morning we would discover fragments of pickled meats, canned goods and such debris, littering the place, although it had been securely locked and barred against human intrusion. It was proposed to remove the provisions and store them elsewhere, but our dear mother, always generous and hospitable, said it was better to endure the loss than risk exposure: if the ghosts were denied this trifling gratification they might set on foot an investigation, which would overthrow our scheme of the division of labor, by diverting the energies of the whole family into the single industry pursued by me—we might all decorate the crossbeams of gibbets. We accepted her decision with filial submission, due to our reverence for her worldly wisdom and the purity of her character.

One night while we were all in the cellar—none dared to enter it alone—engaged in bestowing upon the Mayor of an adjoining town the solemn offices of Christian burial, my mother and the younger children, holding a candle each, while George Henry and I labored with a spade and pick, my sister Mary Maria uttered a shriek and covered her eyes with her hands. We were all dreadfully startled and the Mayor's obsequies were instantly suspended, while with pale faces and in trembling tones we begged her to say what had alarmed her. The younger children were so agitated that they held their candles unsteadily, and the waving shadows of our figures danced with uncouth and grotesque movements on the walls and flung themselves into the most uncanny attitudes. The face of the dead man, now gleaming ghastly in the light, and now extinguished by some floating shadow, appeared at each emergence to have taken on a new and more forbidding expression, a maligner menace. Frightened even more than ourselves by the girl's scream, rats raced in multitudes about the place, squeaking shrilly, or starred the black opacity of some distant corner with steadfast eyes, mere points of green light, matching the faint phosphorescence of decay that filled the half-dug grave and seemed the visible manifestation of that faint odor of mortality which tainted the unwholesome air. The children now sobbed and clung about the limbs of their elders, dropping their candles, and we were near being left in total darkness, except for that sinister light, which slowly welled upward from the disturbed earth and overflowed the edges of the grave like a fountain.

Meanwhile my sister, crouching in the earth that had been thrown out of the excavation, had removed her hands from her face and was staring with expanded eyes into an obscure space between two wine casks.

"There it is!—there it is!" she shrieked, pointing; "God in heaven! can't you see it?"

And there indeed it was!—a human figure, dimly discernible in the gloom—a figure that wavered from side to side as if about to fall, clutching at the wine-casks for support, had stepped unsteadily forward and for one moment stood revealed in the light of our remaining candles; then it surged heavily and fell prone upon the earth. In that moment we had all recognized the figure, the face and bearing of our father—dead these ten months and buried by our own hands!—our father indubitably risen and ghastly drunk!

On the incidents of our precipitate flight from that horrible place—on the extinction of all human sentiment in that tumultuous, mad scramble up the damp and mouldy stairs—slipping, falling, pulling one another down and clambering over one another's back—the lights extinguished, babes trampled beneath the feet of their strong brothers and hurled backward to death by a mother's arm!—on all this I do not dare to dwell. My mother, my eldest brother and sister and I escaped; the others remained below, to perish of their wounds, or of their terror— some, perhaps, by flame. For within an hour we four, hastily gathering together what money and jewels we had and what clothing we could carry, fired the dwelling and fled by its light into the hills. We did not even pause to collect the insurance, and my dear mother said on her death-bed, years afterward in a distant land, that this was the only sin of omission that lay upon her conscience. Her confessor, a holy man, assured her that under the circumstances Heaven would pardon the neglect.

About ten years after our removal from the scenes of my childhood I, then a prosperous forger, returned in disguise to the spot with a view to obtaining, if possible, some treasure belonging to us, which had been buried in the cellar. I may say that I was unsuccessful: the discovery of many human bones in the ruins had set the authorities digging for more. They had found the treasure and had kept it for their honesty. The house had not been rebuilt; the whole suburb was, in fact, a desolation. So many unearthly sights and sounds had been reported thereabout that nobody would live there. As there was none to question nor molest, I resolved to gratify my filial piety by gazing once more upon the face of my beloved father, if indeed our eyes had deceived us and he was still in his grave. I remembered, too, that he had always worn an enormous diamond ring, and never having seen it nor heard of it since his death, I had reason to think he might have been buried in it. Procuring a spade, I soon located the grave in what had been the backyard and began digging. When I had got down about four feet the whole bottom fell out of the grave and I was precipitated into a large drain, falling through a long hole in its crumbling arch. There was no body, nor any vestige of one.

Unable to get out of the excavation, I crept through the drain, and having with some difficulty removed a mass of charred rubbish and blackened masonry that choked it, emerged into what had been that fateful cellar.

All was clear. My father, whatever had caused him to be "taken bad" at his meal (and I think my sainted mother could have thrown some light upon that matter) had indubitably been buried alive. The grave having been accidentally dug above the forgotten drain, and down almost to the crown of its arch, and no coffin having been used, his struggles on reviving had broken the rotten masonry and he had fallen through, escaping finally into the cellar. Feeling that he was not welcome in his own house, yet having no other, he had lived in subterranean seclusion, a witness to our thrift and a pensioner on our food; it was he who had eaten our food; it was he who had drunk our wine—he was no better than a thief! In a moment of intoxication, and feeling, no doubt, that need of companionship which is the one sympathetic link between a drunken man and his race, he had left his place of concealment at a strangely inopportune time, entailing the most deplorable consequences upon those nearest and dearest to him—a blunder that had almost the dignity of crime.

THE BAPTISM OF DOBSHO

It was a wicked thing to do, certainly. I have often regretted it since, and if the opportunity of doing so again were presented I should hesitate a long time before embracing it. But I was young then, and cherished a species of humor which I have since abjured. Still, when I remember the character of the people who were burlesquing and bringing into disrepute the letter and spirit of our holy religion I feel a certain satisfaction in having contributed one feeble effort toward making them ridiculous. In consideration of the little good I may have done in that way, I beg the reader to judge my conceded error as leniently as possible. This is the story.

Some years ago the town of Harding, in Illinois, experienced a "revival of religion," as the people called it. It would have been more accurate and less profane to term it a revival of Rampageanism, for the craze originated in, and was disseminated by, the sect which I will call the Rampagean communion; and most of the leaping and howling was done in that interest. Amongst those who yielded to the influence was my friend Thomas Dobsho. Tom had been a pretty bad sinner in a small way, but he went into this new thing heart and soul. At one of the meetings he made a public confession of more sins than he ever was, or ever could have been guilty of; stopping just short of statutory crimes, and even hinting, significantly, that he could tell a good deal more if he were pressed. He wanted to join the absurd communion the very evening of his conversion. He wanted to join two or three communions. In fact, he was so carried away with his zeal that some of the brethren gave me a hint to take him home; he and I occupied adjoining apartments in the Elephant Hotel.

Tom's fervor, as it happened, came near defeating its own purpose; instead of taking him at once into the fold without reference or "character," which was their usual way, the brethren remembered against him his awful confessions and put him on probation. But after a few weeks, during which he conducted himself like a decent lunatic, it was decided to baptise him along with a dozen other pretty hard cases who had been converted more recently. This sacrilegious ceremony I persuaded myself it was my duty to prevent though I think now I erred as to the means adopted. It was to take place on a Sunday, and on the preceding Saturday I called on the head revivalist, the Rev. Mr. Swin, and craved an interview.

"I come," said I, with simulated reluctance and embarrassment, "in behalf of my friend, Brother Dobsho, to make a very delicate and unusual request. You are, I think, going to baptise him tomorrow, and I trust it will be to him the beginning of a new and better life. But I don't know if you are aware that his family are all Plungers, and that he is himself tainted with the wicked heresy of that sect. So it is. He is, as one might say in secular metaphor, 'on the fence' between their grievous error and the pure faith of your church. It would be most melancholy if he should get down on the wrong side. Although I confess with shame I have not myself embraced the truth, I hope I am not too blind to see where it lies."

"The calamity that you apprehend," said the reverend lout, after solemn reflection, "would indeed seriously affect our friend's interest and endanger his soul. I had not expected Brother Dobsho so soon to give up the good fight."

"I think sir," I replied reflectively, "there is no fear of that if the matter is skilfully managed. He is heartily with you—might I venture to say with us?—on every point but one. He favors immersion! He has been so vile a sinner that he foolishly fears the more simple rite of your church will not make him wet enough. Would you believe it? his uninstructed scruples on the point are so gross and materialistic that he actually suggested soaping himself as a preparatory ceremony! I believe, however, if instead of sprinkling my friend, you would pour a generous basinful of water on his head—but now that I think of it in your enlightening presence I see that such a proceeding is quite out of the question. I fear we must let matters take the usual course, trusting to our later efforts to prevent the backsliding which may result."

The parson rose and paced the floor a moment, then suggested that he'd better see Brother Dobsho, and labor to remove his error. I told him I thought not; I was sure it would not be best. Argument would only confirm him in his prejudices. So it was settled that the subject should not be broached in that quarter. It would have been bad for me if it had been.

When I reflect now upon the guile of that conversation, the falsehood of my representations and the wickedness of my motive I am almost ashamed to proceed with my narrative. Had the minister been other than an arrant humbug, I hope I should never have suffered myself to make him the dupe of a scheme so sacrilegious in itself, and prosecuted with so sinful a disregard of honor.

The memorable Sabbath dawned bright and beautiful. About nine o'clock the cracked old bell, rigged up on struts before the "meeting-house," began to clamor its call to service, and nearly the whole population of Harding took its way to the performance. I had taken the precaution to set my watch fifteen minutes fast. Tom was nervously preparing himself for the ordeal. He fidgeted himself into his best suit an hour before the time, carried his hat about the room in the most aimless and demented way and consulted his watch a hundred times. I was to accompany him to church, and I spent the time fussing about the room, doing the most extraordinary things in the most exasperating manner—in short, keeping up Tom's feverish excitement by every wicked device I could think of. Within a half hour of the real time for service I suddenly yelled out—

"O, I say, Tom; pardon me, but that head of yours is just frightful! Please do let me brush it up a bit!"

Seizing him by the shoulders I thrust him into a chair with his face to the wall, laid hold of his comb and brush, got behind him and went to work. He was trembling like a child, and knew no more what I was doing than if he had been brained. Now, Tom's head was a curiosity. His hair, which was remarkably thick, was like wire. Being cut rather short it stood out all over his scalp like the spines on a porcupine. It had been a favorite complaint of Tom's that he never could do anything to that head. I found no difficulty—I did something to it, though I blush to think what it was. I did something which I feared he might discover if he looked in the mirror, so I carelessly pulled out my watch, sprung it open, gave a start and shouted—

"By Jove! Thomas—pardon the oath—but we're late. Your watch is all wrong; look at mine! Here's your hat, old fellow; come along. There's not a moment to lose!"

Clapping his hat on his head, I pulled him out of the house, with actual violence. In five minutes more we were in the meeting-house with ever so much time to spare.

The services that day, I am told, were specially

interesting and impressive, but I had a good deal else on my mind—was preoccupied, absent, inattentive. They might have varied from the usual profane exhibition in any respect and to any extent, and I should not have observed it. The first thing I clearly perceived was a rank of "converts" kneeling before the "altar," Tom at the left of the line. Then the Rev. Mr. Swin approached him, thoughtfully dipping his fingers into a small earthern bowl of water as if he had just finished dining. I was much affected: I could see nothing distinctly for my tears. My handkerchief was at my face—most of it inside. I was observed to sob spasmodically, and I am abashed to think how many sincere persons mistakenly followed my example.

With some solemn words, the purport of which I did not quite make out, except that they sounded like swearing, the minister stood before Thomas, gave me a glance of intelligence and then with an innocent expression of face, the recollection of which to this day fills me with remorse, spilled, as if by accident, the entire contents of the bowl on the head of my poor friend—that head into the hair of which I had sifted a prodigal profusion of Seidlitz-powders!

I confess it, the effect was magical—anyone who was present would tell you that. Tom's pow simmered—it seethed—it foamed yeastily, and slavered like a mad dog! It steamed and hissed, with angry spurts and flashes! In a second it had grown bigger than a small snowbank, and whiter. It surged, and boiled, and walloped, and overflowed, and sputtered—sent off feathery flakes like down from a shot swan! The froth poured creaming over his face, and got into his eyes. It was the most sinful shampooing of the season!

I cannot relate the commotion this produced, nor would I if I could. As to Tom, he sprang to his feet and staggered out of the house, groping his way between the pews, sputtering strangled profanity and gasping like a stranded fish. The other candidates for baptism rose also, shaking their pates as if to say, "No you don't, my hearty," and left the house in a body. Amidst unbroken silence the minister reascended the pulpit with the empty bowl in his hand, and was first to speak:

"Brethren and sisters," said he with calm, deliberate evenness of tone, "I have held forth in this tabernacle for many more years than I have got fingers and toes, and during that time I have known not guile, nor anger, nor any uncharitableness. As to Henry Barber, who put up this job on me, I judge him not lest I be judged. Let him take *that* and sin no more!"—and he flung the earthern bowl with so true an aim that it was shattered against my skull. The rebuke was not undeserved, I confess, and I trust I have profited by it.

THE HYPNOTIST

By those of my friends who happen to know that I sometimes amuse myself with hypnotism, mind reading and kindred phenomena, I am frequently asked if I have a clear conception of the nature of whatever principle underlies them. To this question I always reply that I neither have nor desire to have. I am no investigator with an ear at the key-hole of Nature's workshop, trying with vulgar curiosity to steal the secrets of her trade. The interests of science are as little to me as mine seem to have been to science.

Doubtless the phenomena in question are simple enough, and in no way transcend our powers of comprehension if only we could find the clew; but for my part I prefer not to find it, for I am of a singularly romantic disposition, deriving more gratification from mystery than from knowledge. It was commonly remarked of me when I was a child that my big blue eyes appeared to have been made rather to look into than look out of—such was their dreamful beauty, and in my frequent periods of abstraction, their indifference to what was going on. In those peculiarities they resembled, I venture to think, the soul which lies behind them, always more intent upon some lovely conception which it has created in its own image than concerned about the laws of nature and the material frame of things. All this, irrelevant and egotistic as it may seem, is related by way of accounting for the meagreness of the light that I am able to throw upon a subject that has engaged so much of my attention, and concerning which there is so keen and general a curiosity. With my powers and opportunities, another person might doubtless have an explanation for much of what I present simply as narrative.

My first knowledge that I possessed unusual powers came to me in my fourteenth year, when at school. Happening one day to have forgotten to bring my noon-day luncheon, I gazed longingly at that of a small girl who was preparing to eat hers. Looking up, her eyes met mine and she seemed unable to withdraw them. After a moment of hesitancy she came forward in an absent kind of way and without a word surrendered her little basket with its tempting contents and walked away. Inexpressibly pleased, I relieved my hunger and destroyed the basket. After that I had not the trouble to bring a luncheon for myself: that little girl was my daily purveyor; and not infrequently in satisfying my simple need from her frugal store I combined pleasure and profit by constraining her attendance at the feast and making misleading proffer of the viands, which eventually I consumed to the last fragment. The girl was always persuaded that she had eaten all herself; and later in the day her tearful complaints of hunger surprised the teacher, entertained the pupils, earned for her the sobriquet of Greedy-Gut and filled me with a peace past understanding.

A disagreeable feature of this otherwise satisfactory condition of things was the necessary secrecy: the transfer of the luncheon, for example, had to be made at some distance from the madding crowd, in a wood; and I blush to think of the many other unworthy subterfuges entailed by the situation. As I was (and am) naturally of a frank and open disposition, these became more and more irksome, and but for the reluctance of my parents to renounce the obvious advantages of the new *régime* I would gladly have reverted to the old. The plan that I finally adopted to free myself from the consequences of my own powers excited a wide and keen interest at the time; and that part of it which consisted in the death of the girl was severely condemned, but it is hardly pertinent to the scope of this narrative.

For some years afterward I had little opportunity to practice hypnotism; such small essays as I made at it were commonly barren of other recognition than solitary confinement on a bread-and-water diet; sometimes, indeed, they elicited nothing better than the cat o'nine-tails. It was when I was about to leave the scene of these small disappointments that my one really important feat was performed.

I had been called into the warden's office and given a suit of civilian's clothing, a trifling sum of money and a great deal of advice, which I am bound to confess was of a much better quality than the clothing. As I was passing out of the gate into the light of freedom I suddenly turned and looking the warden gravely in the eye, soon had him in control.

"You are an ostrich," I said.

At the post-mortem examination the stomach was found to contain a great quantity of indigestible articles mostly of wood or metal. Stuck fast in the œsophagus and constituting, according to the Coroner's jury, the immediate cause of death, one door-knob.

I was by nature a good and affectionate son, but as I took my way into the great world from which I had been so long secluded I could not help remembering that all my misfortunes had flowed like a stream from the niggard economy of my parents in the matter of school luncheons; and I knew of no reason to think they had reformed.

On the road between Succotash Hill and South Asphyxia is a little open field which once contained a shanty known as Pete Gilstrap's Place, where that gentle-man used to murder travelers for a living. The death of Mr. Gilstrap and the diversion of nearly all the travel to another road occurred so nearly at the same time that no one has ever been able to say which was cause and which effect.

Anyhow, the field was now a desolation and the Place had long been burned. It was while going afoot to South Asphyxia, the home of my childhood, that

I found both my parents on their way to the Hill.

They had hitched their team and were eating luncheon under an oak tree in the center of the field. The sight of the luncheon called up painful memories of my school days and roused the sleeping lion in my breast. Approaching the guilty couple, who at once recognized me, I ventured to suggest that I share their hospitality.

"Of this cheer, my son," said the author of my being, with characteristic pomposity, which age had not withered, "there is sufficient for but two; I am not, I hope, insensible to the hunger-light in your eyes, but—"

My father has never completed that sentence; what he mistook for hunger-light was simply the earnest gaze of the hypnotist. In a few seconds he was at my service. A few more sufficed for the lady, and the dictates of a just resentment could be carried into effect. "My former father," I said, "I presume that it is known to you that you and this lady are no longer what you were?"

"I have observed a certain subtle change," was the rather dubious reply of the old gentle-man; "it is perhaps attributable to age."

"It is more than that," I explained; "it goes to character—to species. You and the lady here are, in truth, two *broncos*—wild stallions both, and unfriendly."

"Why, John," exclaimed my dear mother, "you don't mean to say that I am—"

"Madam," I replied, solemnly, fixing my eyes again upon hers, "you are."

Scarcely had the words fallen from my lips when she dropped upon her hands and knees, and backing up to the old man squealed like a demon and delivered a vicious kick upon his shin! An instant later he was himself down on all-fours, headed away from her and flinging his feet at her simultaneously and successively. With equal earnestness but inferior agility, because of her hampering body gear, she plied her own. Their flying legs crossed and mingled in the most bewildering way; their feet sometimes meeting squarely in mid air, their bodies thrust forward, falling flat upon the ground and for a moment helpless. On recovering themselves they would resume the combat, uttering their frenzy in the nameless sounds of the furious brutes which they believed themselves to be—the whole region rang with their clamor! Round and round they wheeled, the blows of their feet falling "like lightnings from the mountain cloud." They plunged and reared backward upon their knees, struck savagely at each other with awkward descending blows of both fists at once, and dropped again upon their hands as if unable to maintain the upright position of the body. Grass and pebbles were torn from the soil by hands and feet; clothing, hair, faces inexpressibly defiled with dust and blood. Wild, inarticulate screams of rage attested the delivery of the blows; groans, grunts and gasps their receipt. Nothing more truly military was ever seen at Gettysburg or Waterloo: the valor of my dear parents in the hour of danger can never cease to be to me a source of pride and gratification. At the end of it all two battered, tattered, bloody and fragmentary vestiges of mortality attested the solemn fact that the author of the strife was an orphan.

Arrested for provoking a breach of the peace, I was, and have ever since been, tried in the Court of Technicalities and Continuances whence, after fifteen years of proceedings, my attorney is moving heaven and earth to get the case taken to the Court of Remandment for New Trials.

Such are a few of my principal experiments in the mysterious force or agency known as hypnotic suggestion. Whether or not it could be employed by a bad man for an unworthy purpose I am unable to say.

MR. MASTHEAD, JOURNALIST

While I was in Kansas I purchased a weekly newspaper—the *Claybank Thundergust of Reform.* This paper had never paid its expenses; it had ruined four consecutive publishers; but my brother-in-law, Mr. Jefferson Scandril, of Weedhaven, was going to run for the Legislature, and I naturally desired his defeat; so it became necessary to have an organ in Claybank to assist in his political extinction. When the establishment came into my hands, the editor was a fellow who had "opinions," and him I at once discharged with an admonition. I had some difficulty in procuring a successor; every man in the county applied for the place. I could not appoint one without having to fight a majority of the others, and was eventually compelled to write to a friend at Warm Springs, in the adjoining State of Missouri, to send me an editor from abroad whose instalment at the helm of manifest destiny could have no local significance.

The man he sent me was a frowsy, seedy fellow, named Masthead—not larger, apparently, than a boy of sixteen years, though it was difficult to say from the outside how much of him was editor and how much cast-off clothing, for in the matter of apparel he had acted upon his favorite professional maxim, and "sunk the individual;" his attire—eminently eclectic, and in a sense international—quite overcame him at all points. However, as my friend had assured me he was "a graduate of one of the largest institutions in his native State," I took him in and bought a pen for him. My instructions to him were brief and simple.

"Mr. Masthead," said I, "it is the policy of the *Thundergust* first, last, and all the time, in this world and the next, to resent the intrusion of Mr. Jefferson Scandril into politics."

The first thing the little rascal did was to write a withering leader denouncing Mr. Scandril as a "demagogue, the degradation of whose political opinions was only equaled by the disgustfulness of the family connections of which those opinions were the spawn!"

I hastened to point out to Mr. Masthead that it had never been the policy of the *Thundergust* to attack the family relations of an offensive candidate, although this was not strictly true.

"I am very sorry," he replied, running his head up out of his clothes till it towered as much as six inches above the table at which he sat; "no offense, I hope."

"Oh, none in the world," said I, as carelessly as I could manage it; "only I don't think it a legitimate—that is, an effective, method of attack."

"Mr. Johnson," said he—I was passing as

Johnson at that time, I remember—"Mr. Johnson, I think it is an effective method. Personally I might perhaps prefer another line of argument in this particular case, and personally perhaps you might; but in our profession personal considerations must be blown to the winds of the horizon; we must sink the individual. In opposing the election of your relative, sir, you have set the seal of your heavy displeasure upon the sin of nepotism, and for this I respect you; nepotism must be got under! But in the display of Roman virtues, sir, we must go the whole hog. When in the interest of public morality"— Mr. Masthead was now gesticulating earnestly with the sleeves of his coat—"Virginius stabbed his daughter, was he influenced by personal considerations? When Curtius leaped into the yawning gulf, did he not sink the individual?"

I admitted that he did, but feeling in a contentious mood, prolonged the discussion by leisurely loading and capping a revolver; but, prescient of my argument, Mr. Masthead avoided refutation by hastily adjourning the debate. I sent him a note that evening, filling-in a few of the details of the policy that I had before sketched in outline. Amongst other things I submitted that it would be better for us to exalt Mr. Scandril's opponent than to degrade himself. To this Mr. Masthead reluctantly assented— "sinking the individual," he reproachfully explained, "in the dependent employee—the powerless bondsman!" The next issue of the *Thundergust* contained, under the heading, "Invigorating Zephyrs," the following editorial article:

"Last week we declared our unalterable opposition to the candidacy of Mr. Jefferson Scandril, and gave reasons for the faith that is in us. For the first time in its history this paper made a clear, thoughtful, and adequate avowal and exposition of eternal principle! Abandoning for the present the stand we then took, let us trace the antecedents of Mr. Scandril's opponent up to their source. It has been urged against Mr. Broskin that he spent some years of his life in the lunatic asylum at Warm Springs, in the adjoining commonwealth of Missouri. This cuckoo cry—raised though it is by dogs of political darkness—we shall not stoop to controvert, for it is accidentally true; but next week we shall show, as by the stroke of an enchanter's wand, that this great statesman's detractors would probably not derive any benefits from a residence in the same institution, their mental aberration being rottenly incurable!"

I thought this rather strong and not quite to the point; but Masthead said it was a fact that our candidate, who was very little known in Claybank, had "served a term" in the Warm Springs asylum, and the issue must be boldly met—that evasion and denial were but forms of prostration beneath the iron wheels of Truth! As he said this he seemed to inflate and expand so as almost to fill his clothes, and the fire of his eye somehow burned into me an impression—

since effaced—that a just cause is not imperiled by a trifling concession to fact. So, leaving the matter quite in my editor's hands I went away to keep some important engagements, the paragraph having involved me in several duels with the friends of Mr. Broskin. I thought it rather hard that I should have to defend my new editor's policy against the supporters of my own candidate, particularly as I was clearly in the right and they knew nothing whatever about the matter in dispute, not one of them having ever before so much as heard of the now famous Warm Springs asylum. But I would not shirk even the humblest journalistic duty; I fought these fellows and acquitted myself as became a man of letters and a politician. The hurts I got were some time healing, and in the interval every prominent member of my party who came to Claybank to speak to the people regarded it as a simple duty to call first at my house, make a tender inquiry as to the progress of my recovery and leave a challenge. My physician forbade me to read a line of anything; the consequence was that Masthead had it all his own way with the paper. In looking over the old files now, I find that he devoted his entire talent and all the space of the paper, including what had been the advertising columns, to confessing that our candidate had been an inmate of a lunatic asylum, and contemptuously asking the opposing party what they were going to do about it.

All this time Mr. Broskin made no sign; but when the challenges became intolerable I indignantly instructed Mr. Masthead to whip round to the other side and support my brother-in-law. Masthead "sank the individual," and duly announced, with his accustomed frankness, our change of policy. Then Mr. Broskin came down to Claybank—to thank me! He was a fine, respectable-looking gentleman, and impressed me very favorably. But Masthead was in when he called, and the effect upon *him* was different. He shrank into a mere heap of old clothes, turned white, and chattered his teeth. Noting this extraordinary behavior, I at once sought an explanation.

"Mr. Broskin," said I, with a meaning glance at the trembling editor, "from certain indications I am led to fear that owing to some mistake we may have been doing you an injustice. May I ask you if you were really ever in the Lunatic asylum at Warm Springs, Missouri?"

"For three years," he replied, quietly, "I was the physician in charge of that institution. Your son"—turning to Masthead, who was flying all sorts of colors—"was, if I mistake not, one of my patients. I learn that a few weeks ago a friend of yours, named Norton, secured the young man's release upon your promise to take care of him yourself in future. I hope that home associations have improved the poor fellow. It's very sad!"

It was indeed. Norton was the name of the man to whom I had written for an editor, and who had sent me one! Norton was ever an obliging fellow.

THE BUBBLE REPUTATION

How Another Man's Was Sought and Pricked

It was a stormy night in the autumn of 1930. The hour was about eleven. San Francisco lay in darkness, for the laborers at the gas works had struck and destroyed the company's property because a newspaper to which a cousin of the manager was a subscriber had censured the course of a potato merchant related by marriage to a member of the Knights of Leisure. Electric lights had not at that period been reinvented. The sky was filled with great masses of black cloud which, driven rapidly across the star-fields by winds unfelt on the earth and momentarily altering their fantastic forms, seemed instinct with a life and activity of their own and endowed with awful powers of evil, to the exercise of which they might at any time set their malignant will.

An observer standing, at this time, at the corner of Paradise avenue and Great White Throne walk in Sorrel Hill cemetery would have seen a human figure moving among the graves toward the Superintendent's residence. Dimly and fitfully visible in the intervals of thinner gloom, this figure had a most uncanny amd disquieting aspect. A long black cloak shrouded it from neck to heel. Upon its head was a slouch hat, pulled down across the forehead and almost concealing the face, which was further hidden by a half-mask, only the beard being occasionally visible as the head was lifted partly above the collar of the cloak. The man wore upon his feet jack-boots whose wide, funnel-shaped legs had settled down in many a fold and crease about his ankles, as could be seen whenever accident parted the bottom of the cloak. His arms were concealed, but sometimes he stretched out the right to steady himself by a headstone as he crept stealthily but blindly over the uneven ground. At such times a close scrutiny of the hand would have disclosed in the palm the hilt of a poniard, the blade of which lay along the wrist, hidden in the sleeve. In short, the man's garb, his movements, the hour—everything proclaimed him a reporter.

But what did he there?

On the morning of that day the editor of the *Daily Malefactor* had touched the button of a bell numbered 216 and in response to the summons Mr. Longbo Spittleworth, reporter, had been shot into the room out of an inclined tube.

"I understand," said the editor, "that you are 216—am I right?"

"That," said the reporter, catching his breath and adjusting his clothing, both somewhat disordered by the celerity of his flight through the tube— "that is my number."

"Information has reached us," continued the editor, "that the Superintendent of the Sorrel Hill cemetery—one Inhumio, whose very name suggests inhumanity—is guilty of the grossest outrages in the administration of the great trust confided to his hands by the sovereign people."

"The cemetery is private property," faintly suggested 216.

"It is alleged," continued the great man, disdaining to notice the interruption, "that in violation of popular rights he refuses to permit his accounts to be inspected by representatives of the press."

"Under the law, you know, he is responsible to the directors of the cemetery company," the reporter ventured to interject.

"They say," pursued the editor, heedless, "that the inmates are in many cases badly lodged and insufficiently clad, and that in consequence they are usually cold. It is asserted that they are never fed—except to the worms. Statements have been made to the effect that males and females are permitted to occupy the same quarters, to the incalculable detriment of public morality. Many clandestine villainies are alleged of this fiend in human shape, and it is desirable that his underground methods be unearthed in the *Malefactor.* If he resists we will drag his family skeleton from the privacy of his domestic closet. There is money in it for the paper, fame for you—are you ambitious, 216?"

"I am—bitious."

"Go, then," cried the editor, rising and waving his hand imperiously—"go and 'seek the bubble reputation'."

"The bubble shall be sought," the young man replied, and leaping into a man-hole in the floor, disappeared. A moment later the editor, who after dismissing his subordinate, had stood motionless, as if lost in thought, sprang suddenly to the man-hole and shouted down it: "Hello, 216?"

"Aye, aye, sir," came up a faint and far reply.

"About that 'bubble reputation'—you understand, I suppose, that the reputation which you are to seek is that of the other man."

In the execution of his duty, in the hope of his employer's approval, in the costume of his profession, Mr. Longbo Spittleworth, otherwise known as 216, has already occupied a place in the mind's eye of the intelligent reader. Alas for poor Mr. Inhumio!

A few days after these events that fearless, independent and enterprising guardian and guide of the public, the San Francisco *Daily Malefactor,* contained a whole-page article whose headlines are here presented with some necessary typographical mitigation:

"Hell Upon Earth! Corruption Rampant in the Management of the Sorrel Hill Cemetery. The Sacred City of the Dead in the Leprous Clutches of a Demon in Human Form. Fiendish Atrocities Committed in 'God's Acre.' The Holy Dead Thrown around Loose. Fragments of Mothers. Segregation of a Beautiful Young Lady Who in Life Was the Light of a Happy Household. A Superintendent Who Is an Ex-Convict. How He Murdered His Neighbor to Start the Cemetery. He Buries His Own Dead Elsewhere. Extraordinary Insolence to a Representative of the Public Press. Little Eliza's Last Words: 'Mamma, Feed Me to the Pigs.' A Moonshiner Who Runs an Illicit Bone-Button Factory in One Corner of the Grounds. Buried Head Downward. Revolting Mausoleistic Orgies. Dancing on the Dead. Devilish Mutilation—a Pile of Late Lamented Noses and Sainted Ears. No Separation of the Sexes; Petitions for Chaperons Unheeded. 'Veal' as Supplied to the Superintendent's Employees. A Miscreant's Record from His Birth. Disgusting Subserviency of Our Contemporaries and Strong Indications of Collusion. Nameless Abnormalities. Doubled Up Like a Nut-Cracker. 'Wasn't Planted White.' Horribly Significant Reduction in the Price of Lard. The Question of the Hour: Whom Do You Fry Your Doughnuts In?"

THE APPLICANT

Pushing his adventurous shins through the deep snow that had fallen overnight, and encouraged by the glee of his little sister, following in the open way that he made, a sturdy small boy, the son of Grayville's most distinguished citizen, struck his foot against something of which there was no visible sign on the surface of the snow. It is the purpose of this narrative to explain how it came to be there.

No one who has had the advantage of passing through Grayville by day can have failed to observe the large stone building crowning the low hill to the north of the railway station—that is to say, to the right in going toward Great Mowbray. It is a somewhat dull-looking edifice, of the Early Comatose order, and appears to have been designed by an architect who shrank from publicity, and although unable to conceal his work—even compelled, in this instance, to set it on an eminence in the sight of men—did what he honestly could to insure it against a second look. So far as concerns its outer and visible aspect, the Abersush Home for Old Men is unquestionably inhospitable to human attention. But it is a building of great magnitude, and cost its benevolent founder the profit of many a cargo of the teas and silks and spices that his ships brought up from the under-world when he was in trade in Boston; though the main expense was its endowment. Altogether, this reckless person had robbed his heirs-at-law of no less a sum than half a million dollars and flung it away in riotous giving. Possibly it was with a view to get out of sight of the silent big witness to his extravagance that he shortly afterward disposed of all his Grayville property that remained to him, turned his back upon the scene of his prodigality and went off across the sea in one of his own ships. But the gossips who got their inspiration most directly from Heaven declared that he went in search of a wife—a theory not easily reconciled with that of the village humorist, who solemnly averred that the bachelor philanthropist had departed this life (left Grayville, to wit) because the marriageable maidens had made it too hot to hold him. However this may have been, he had not returned, and although at long intervals there had come to Grayville, in a desultory way, vague rumors of his wanderings in strange lands, no one seemed certainly to know about him, and to the new generation he was no more than a name. But from above the portal of the Home for Old Men the name shouted in stone.

Despite its unpromising exterior, the Home is a fairly commodious place of retreat from the ills that its inmates have incurred by being poor and old and men. At the time embraced in this brief chronicle they were in number about a score, but in acerbity, querulousness, and general ingratitude they could hardly be reckoned at fewer than a hundred; at least that was the estimate of the superintendent, Mr. Silas Tilbody. It was Mr. Tilbody's steadfast conviction that always, in admitting new old men to replace those who had gone to another and a better Home, the trustees had distinctly in will the infraction of his peace, and the trial of his patience. In truth, the longer the institution was connected with him, the stronger was his feeling that the founder's scheme of benevolence was sadly impaired by providing any inmates at all. He had not much imagination, but with what he had he was addicted to the reconstruction of the Home for Old Men into a kind of "castle in Spain," with himself as castellan, hospitably entertaining about a score of sleek and prosperous middle-aged gentlemen, consummately good-humored and civilly willing to pay for their board and lodging. In this revised project of philanthropy the trustees, to whom he was indebted for his office and responsible for his conduct, had not the happiness to appear. As to them, it was held by the village humorist aforementioned that in their management of the great charity Providence had thoughtfully supplied an incentive to thrift. With the inference which he expected to be drawn from that view we have nothing to do; it had neither support nor denial from the inmates, who certainly were most concerned. They lived out their little remnant of life, crept into graves neatly numbered, and were succeeded by other old men as like them as could be desired by the Adversary of Peace. If the Home was a place of punishment for the sin of unthrift the veteran offenders sought justice with a persistence that attested the sincerity of their penitence. It is to one of these that the reader's attention is now invited.

In the matter of attire this person was not altogether engaging. But for this season, which was midwinter, a careless observer might have looked upon him as a clever device of the husbandman indisposed to share the fruits of his toil with the crows that toil not, neither spin—an error that might not have been dispelled without longer and closer observation than he seemed to court; for his progress up Abersush Street, toward the Home in the gloom of the winter evening, was not visibly faster than what might have been expected of a scarecrow blessed with youth, health, and discontent. The man was indisputably ill-clad, yet not without a certain fitness and good taste, withal; for he was obviously an applicant for admittance to the Home, where poverty was a qualification. In the army of indigence the uniform is rags; they serve to distinguish the rank and file from the recruiting officers.

As the old man, entering the gate of the grounds, shuffled up the broad walk, already white with the fast-falling snow, which from time to time he feebly shook from its various coigns of vantage on his person, he came under inspection of the large globe lamp that burned always by night over the great door of the building. As if unwilling to incur its revealing beams, he turned to the left and, passing a considerable distance along the face of the building, rang at a smaller door emitting a dimmer ray that came from within, through the fanlight, and expended itself incuriously overhead. The door was opened by no less a personage than the great Mr. Tilbody himself. Observing his visitor, who at once uncovered, and somewhat shortened the radius of the permanent curvature of his back, the great man gave visible token of neither surprise nor displeasure. Mr. Tilbody was, indeed, in an uncommonly good humor, a phenomenon ascribable doubtless to the cheerful influence of the season; for this was Christmas Eve, and the morrow would be that blessed 365th part of the year that all Christian souls set apart for mighty feats of goodness and joy. Mr. Tilbody was so full of the spirit of the season that his fat face and pale blue eyes, whose ineffectual fire served to distinguish it from an untimely summer squash, effused so genial a glow that it seemed a pity that he could not have lain down in it, basking in the consciousness of his own identity. He was hatted, booted, overcoated, and umbrellaed, as became a person who was about to expose himself to the night and the storm on an errand of charity; for Mr. Tilbody had just parted from his wife and children to go "down town" and purchase the wherethal to confirm the annual falsehood about the ınch-bellied saint who frequents the chimneys to reward little boys and girls who are good, and especially truthful. So he did not invite the old man in, but saluted him cheerily:

"Hello! just in time; a moment later and you would have missed me. Come, I have no time to waste; we'll walk a little way together."

"Thank you," said the old man, upon whose thin and white but not ignoble face the light from the open door showed an expression that was perhaps disappointment; "but if the trustees—if my application—"

"The trustees," Mr. Tilbody said, closing more doors than one, and cutting off two kinds of light, "have agreed that your application disagrees with them."

Certain sentiments are inappropriate to Christmastide, but Humor, like Death, has all seasons for his own.

"Oh, my God!" cried the old man, in so thin and husky a tone that the invocation was anything but impressive, and to at least one of his two auditors sounded, indeed, somewhat ludicrous. To the Other—but that is a matter which laymen are devoid of the light to expound.

"Yes," continued Mr. Tilbody, accommodating his gait to that of his companion, who was mechanically, and not very successfully, retracing the track that he had made through the snow; "they have decided that, under the circumstances—under the very peculiar circumstances, you understand—it would be inexpedient to admit you. As superintendent and

—100—

ex officio secretary of the honorable board"— as Mr. Tilbody "read his title clear" the magnitude of the big building, seen through its veil of falling snow, appeared to suffer somewhat in comparison—"it is my duty to inform you that, in the words of Deacon Byram, the chairman, your presence in the Home would—under the circumstances—be peculiarly embarrassing. I felt it my duty to submit to the honorable board the statement that you made to me yesterday of your needs, your physical condition, and the trials which it has pleased Providence to send upon you in your very proper effort to present your claims in person; but after careful, and I may say prayerful, consideration of your case—with something too, I trust, of the large charitableness appropriate to the season—it was decided that we would not be justified in doing anything likely to impair the usefulness of the institution intrusted (under Providence) to our care."

They had now passed out of the grounds; the street lamp opposite the gate was dimly visible through the snow. Already the old man's former track was obliterated, and he seemed uncertain as to which way he should go. Mr. Tilbody had drawn a little away from him, but paused and turned half toward him, apparently reluctant to forego the continuing opportunity.

"Under the circumstances," he resumed, "the decision—"

But the old man was inaccessible to the suasion

of his verbosity; he had crossed the street into a vacant lot and was going forward, rather deviously toward nowhere in particular—which, he having nowhere in particular to go to, was not so reasonless a proceeding as it looked.

And that is how it happened that the next morning, when the church bells of all Grayville were ringing with an added unction appropriate to the day, the sturdy little son of Deacon Byram, breaking a way through the snow to the place of worship, struck his foot against the body of Amasa Abersush, philanthropist.

MY FAVORITE MURDER

Having murdered my mother under circumstances of singular atrocity, I was arrested and put upon my trial, which lasted seven years. In charging the jury, the judge of the Court of Acquittal remarked that it was one of the most ghastly crimes that he had ever been called upon to explain away.

At this, my attorney rose and said:

"May it please your Honor, crimes are ghastly or agreeable only by comparison. If you were familiar with the details of my client's previous murder of his uncle you would discern in his later offense (if offense it may be called) something in the nature of tender forbearance and filial consideration for the feelings of the victim. The appalling ferocity of the former assassination was indeed inconsistent with any hypothesis but that of guilt; and had it not been for the fact that the honorable judge before whom he was tried was the president of a life insurance company that took risks on hanging, and in which my client held a policy, it is hard to see how he could decently have been acquitted. If your Honor would like to hear about it for instruction and guidance of your Honor's mind, this unfortunate man, my client, will consent to give himself the pain of relating it under oath."

The district attorney said: "Your Honor, I object. Such a statement would be in the nature of evidence, and the testimony in this case is closed. The prisoner's statement should have been introduced three years ago, in the spring of 1881."

"In a statutory sense," said the judge, "you are right, and in the Court of Objections and Technicalities you would get a ruling in your favor. But not in a Court of Acquittal. The objection is overruled."

"I except," said the district attorney.

"You cannot do that," the judge said. "I must remind you that in order to take an exception you must first get this case transferred for a time to the Court of Exceptions on a formal motion duly supported by affidavits. A motion to that effect by your predecessor in office was denied by me during the first year of this trial. Mr. Clerk, swear the prisoner."

The customary oath having been administered, I made the following statement, which impressed the judge with so strong a sense of the comparative triviality of the offense for which I was on trial that he made no further search for mitigating circumstances, but simply instructed the jury to acquit, and I left the court, without a stain upon my reputation:

"I was born in 1856 in Kalamakee, Mich., of honest and reputable parents, one of whom Heaven has mercifully spared to comfort me in my later years. In 1867 the family came to California and settled near Nigger Head, where my father opened a road agency and prospered beyond the dreams of avarice. He was a reticent, saturnine man then, though his increasing years have now somewhat relaxed the austerity of his disposition, and I believe that nothing but his memory of the sad event for which I am now on trial prevents him from manifesting a genuine hilarity.

"Four years after we had set up the road agency an itinerant preacher came along, and having no other way to pay for the night's lodging that we gave him, favored us with an exhortation of such power that, praise God, we were all converted to religion. My father at once sent for his brother, the Hon. William Ridley of Stockton, and on his arrival turned over the agency to him, charging him nothing for the franchise nor plant—the latter consisting of a Winchester rifle, a sawed-off shotgun, and an assortment of masks made out of flour sacks. The family then moved to Ghost Rock and opened a dance house. It was called 'The Saints' Rest Hurdy-Gurdy,' and the proceedings each night began with prayer. It was there that my now sainted mother, by her grace in the dance, acquired the *sobriquet* of 'The Bucking Walrus.'

"In the fall of '75 I had occasion to visit Coyote, on the road to Mahala, and took the stage at Ghost Rock. There were four other passengers. About three miles beyond Nigger Head, persons whom I identified as my Uncle William and his two sons held up the stage. Finding nothing in the express box, they went through the passengers. I acted a most honorable part in the affair, placing myself in line with the others, holding up my hands and permitting myself to be deprived of forty dollars and a gold watch. From my behavior no one could have suspected that I knew the gentlemen who gave the entertainment. A few days later, when I went to Nigger Head and asked for the return of my money and watch my uncle and cousins swore they knew nothing of the matter, and they affected a belief that my father and I had done the job ourselves in dishonest violation of commercial good faith. Uncle William even threatened to retaliate by starting an opposition dance house at Ghost Rock. As 'The Saints' Rest' had become rather unpopular, I saw that this would assuredly ruin it and prove a paying enterprise, so I told my uncle that I was willing to overlook the past if he would take me into the scheme and keep the partnership a secret from my father. This fair offer he rejected, and I then perceived that it would be better and more satisfactory if he were dead.

"My plans to that end were soon perfected, and communicating them to my dear parents I had the gratification of receiving their approval. My father said he was proud of me, and my mother promised that although her religion forbade her to assist in taking human life I should have the advantage of her prayers for my success. As a preliminary measure looking to my security in case of detection I made an application for membership in that powerful order, the Knights of Murder, and in due course was received as a member of the Ghost Rock commandery. On the day that my probation ended I was for the first time permitted to inspect the records of the order and learn who belonged to it, all the rites of initiation having been conducted in masks. Fancy my delight when, in looking over the roll of membership, I found the third name to be that of my uncle, who indeed was junior vice-chancellor of the order! Here was an opportunity exceeding my wildest dreams—to murder I could add insubordination and treachery. It was what my good mother would have called 'a special Providence.'

"At about this time something occurred which caused my cup of joy, already full, to overflow on all sides, a circular cataract of bliss.

Three men, strangers in that locality, were arrested for the stage robbery in which I had lost my money and watch. They were brought to trial and, despite my efforts to clear them and fasten the guilt upon three of the most respectable and worthy citizens of Ghost Rock, convicted on the clearest proof. The murder would now be as wanton and reasonless as I could wish.

"One morning I shouldered my Winchester rifle, and going over to my uncle's house, near Nigger Head, asked my Aunt Mary, his wife, if he were at home, adding that I had come to kill him. My aunt replied with her peculiar smile that so many gentlemen called on that errand and were afterward carried away without having performed it that I must excuse her for doubting my good faith in the matter. She said I did not look as if I would kill anybody, so as a proof of good faith I leveled my rifle and wounded a Chinaman who happened to be passing the house. She said she knew whole families that could do a thing of that kind, but Bill Ridley was a horse of another color. She said, however, that I would find him over on the other side of the creek in the sheep lot; and she added that she hoped the best man would win.

"My Aunt Mary was one of the most fair-minded women that I have ever met.

"I found my uncle down on his knees engaged in skinning a sheep. Seeing that he had neither gun nor pistol handy I had not the heart to shoot him, so I approached him, greeted him pleasantly and struck him a powerful blow on the head with the butt of my rifle. I have a very good delivery and Uncle William lay down on his side, then rolled over on his back, spread out his fingers and shivered. Before he could recover the use of his limbs I seized the knife that he had been using and cut his hamstrings. You know, doubtless, that when you sever the *tendo Achillis* the patient has no further use of his leg; it is just the same as if he had no leg. Well, I parted them both, and when he revived he was at my service. As soon as he comprehended the situation, he said:

"'Samuel, you have got the drop on me and can afford to be generous. I have only one thing to ask of you, and that is that you carry me to the house and finish me in the bosom of my family.'

I told him I thought that a pretty reasonable request and I would do so if he would let me put him into a wheat sack; he would be easier to carry that way and if we were seen by the neighbors *en route* it would cause less remark. He agreed to that, and going to the barn I got a sack. This, however, did not fit him; it was too short and much wider than he; so I bent his legs, forced his knees up against his breast and got him into it that way, tying the sack above his head. He was a heavy man and I had all that I could do to get him on my back, but I staggered along for some distance until I came to a swing that some of the children had suspended to the branch of an oak.

"Here I laid him down and sat upon him to rest, and the sight of the rope gave me a happy inspiration. In twenty minutes my uncle, still in the sack, swung free to the sport of the wind.

"I had taken down the rope, tied one end tightly about the mouth of the bag, thrown the other across the limb and hauled him up about five feet from the ground. Fastening the other end of the rope also about the mouth of the sack, I had the satisfaction to see my uncle converted into a large, fine pendulum. I must add that he was not himself entirely aware of the nature of the change that he had undergone in his relation to the exterior world, though in justice to a good man's memory I ought to say that I do not think he would in any case have wasted much of my time in vain remonstrance.

"Uncle William had a ram that was famous in all that region as a fighter. It was in a state of chronic constitutional indignation. Some deep disappointment in early life had soured its disposition and it had declared war upon the whole world. To say that it would butt anything accessible is but faintly to express the nature and scope of its military activity: the universe was its antagonist; its methods that of a projectile. It fought like the angels and devils, in mid-air, cleaving the atmosphere like a bird, describing a parabolic curve and descending upon its victim at just the exact angle of incidence to make the most of its velocity and weight. Its momentum, calculated in foot-tons, was something incredible. It had been seen to destroy a four-year-old bull by a single impact upon that animal's gnarly forehead. No stone wall had ever been known to resist its downward swoop; there were no trees tough enough to stay it; it would splinter them into matchwood and defile their leafy honors in the dust. This irascible and implacable brute—this incarnate thunderbolt—this monster of the upper deep, I had seen reposing in the shade of an adjacent tree, dreaming dreams of conquest and glory. It was with a view to summoning it forth to the field of honor that I suspended its master in the manner described.

"Having completed my preparations, I imparted to the avuncular pendulum a gentle oscillation, and retiring to cover behind a contiguous rock, lifted up my voice in a long rasping cry whose diminishing final note was drowned in a noise like that of a swearing cat, which emanated from the sack. Instantly that formidable sheep was upon its feet and had taken in the military situation at a glance. In a few moments it had approached, stamping, to within fifty yards of the swinging foeman, who, now retreating and anon advancing, seemed to invite the fray. Suddenly I saw the beast's head drop earthward as if depressed by the weight of its enormous horns; then a dim, white, wavy streak of sheep prolonged itself from that spot in a generally horizontal direction to within about four yards of a point immediately beneath the enemy. There it struck sharply upward, and before it had faded from my gaze at the place whence it had set out I heard a horrid thump and a piercing scream, and my poor uncle shot forward, with a slack rope higher than the limb to which he was attached. Here the rope tautened with a jerk, arresting his flight, and back he swung in a breathless curve to the other end of his arc. The ram had fallen, a heap of indistinguishable legs, wool and horns, but pulling itself together and dodging as its antagonist swept downward it retired at random, alternately shaking its head and stamping its fore-feet. When it had backed about the same distance as that from which it had delivered the assault it paused again, bowed its head as if in prayer for victory and again shot forward, dimly visible as before—a prolonging white streak with monstrous undulations, ending with a sharp ascension. Its course this time was at a right angle to its former one, and its impatience so great that it struck the enemy before he had nearly reached the lowest point of his arc. In consequence he went flying round and round in a horizontal circle whose radius was about equal to half the length of the rope, which I forgot to say was nearly twenty feet long. His shrieks, *crescendo* in approach and *diminuendo* in recession, made the rapidity of his revolution more obvious to the ear than to the eye. He had evidently not yet been struck in a vital spot. His posture in the sack and the distance from the ground at which he hung compelled the ram to operate upon his lower extremities and the end of his back. Like a plant that has struck its root into some poisonous mineral, my poor uncle was dying slowly upward.

"After delivering its second blow the ram had not again retired. The fever of battle burned hot in its heart; its brain was intoxicated with the wine of strife. Like a pugilist who in his rage forgets his skill and fights ineffectively at half-arm's length, the angry beast endeavored to reach its fleeting foe by awkard vertical leaps as he passed overhead, sometimes, indeed, succeeding in striking him feebly, but more frequently overthrown by its own misguided eagerness. But as the impetus was exhausted and the man's circles narrowed in scope and diminished in speed, bringing him nearer to the ground, these tactics produced better results, eliciting a superior quality of screams, which I greatly enjoyed.

"Suddenly, as if the bugles had sung truce, the ram suspended hostilities and walked away, thoughtfully wrinkling and smoothing its great aquiline nose, and occasionally cropping a bunch of grass and slowly munching it. It seemed to have tired of war's alarms and resolved to beat the sword into a plowshare and cultivate the arts of peace. Steadily it held its course away from the field of fame until it had gained a distance of nearly a quarter of a mile. There it stopped and stood with its rear to the foe, chewing its cud and apparently half asleep. I observed, however, an occasional slight turn of its head, as if its apathy were more affected than real.

"Meantime Uncle William's shrieks had abated with his motion, and nothing was heard from him but long, low moans, and at long intervals my name, uttered in pleading tones exceedingly grateful to my ear. Evidently the man had not the faintest notion of what was being done to him, and was inexpressibly terrified. When Death comes cloaked in mystery he is terrible indeed. Little by little my uncle's oscillations diminished, and finally he hung motionless. I went to him and was about to give him the *coup de grâce,* when I heard and felt a succession of smart shocks which shook the ground like a series of light earthquakes, and turning in the direction of the ram, saw a long cloud of dust approaching me with inconceivable rapidity and alarming effect! At a distance of some thirty yards away it stopped short, and from the near end of it rose into the air what I at first thought a great white bird. Its ascent was so smooth and easy and regular that I could not realize its extraordinary celerity, and was lost in admiration of its grace. To this day the impression remains that it was a slow, deliberate movement, the ram—for it was that animal—being upborne by some power other than its own impetus, and supported through the successive stages of its flight with infinite tenderness and care. My eyes followed its progress through the air with unspeakable pleasure, all the greater by contrast with my former terror of its approach by land. Onward and upward the noble animal sailed, its head bent down almost between its knees, its fore-feet thrown back, its hinder legs trailing to rear like the legs of a soaring heron.

"At a height of forty or fifty feet, as fond recollection presents it to view, it attained its zenith and appeared to remain an instant stationary; then, tilting suddenly forward without altering the relative position of its parts, it shot downward on a steeper and steeper course with augmenting velocity, passed immediately above me with a noise like the rush of a cannon shot and struck my poor uncle almost squarely on the top of the head! So frightful was the impact that not only the man's neck was broken, but the rope too; and the body of the deceased, forced against the earth, was crushed to pulp beneath the awful front of that meteoric sheep! The concussion stopped all the clocks between Lone Hand and Dutch Dan's, and Professor Davidson, a distinguished authority in matters seismic, who happened to be in the vicinity, promptly explained that the vibrations were from north to southwest.

"Altogether, I cannot help thinking that in point of artistic atrocity my murder of Uncle William has seldom been excelled."

THE RESURRECTION OF DEAD DOGS

An Afterword by Carl Japikse

I had just finished editing these stories for publication when an odd thing occurred. The doorbell rang. I went to open it, thinking it was the postman, who only rings once. But it was not. No one was there, nor anywhere in sight. Yet I was not entirely alone on the stoop. Directly in front of me was a neatly wrapped package, about the size of a family Bible, deposited upon the welcome mat.

I picked up the package and examined it. It was clearly addressed to me, and yet there was no return address. Nor was there any sign of postage, nor any indication that it had been brought by a parcel service. As far as I could determine, it might as well have been brought by stork. Perhaps it was.

I listened to the package, to make sure it was not a bomb, but all I could hear was the sound of some distant ocean. So I took the package inside and laid it on my work table. I walked around it several times, wondering what to do. At last, I hit upon a plan, got out my scissors, and opened it.

Inside was a thin sheaf of papers, a letter of

some kind. Yet it was not actually a letter, as it was not addressed to me, nor anyone in particular. It was more of an open declaration, written to whomever might happen to read it.

The treatise was handwritten, not typed; yet the penmanship was so perfect and legible that I knew in an instant that the letter must have been written a long time ago. I leafed through the pages, until I came to the final one. I was correct: it had been written decades earlier, about the time of his disappearance, by none other than Ambrose Bierce. I reprint this remarkable document here in its entirety:

"I do not presume to know who will eventually read this final farewell, but I have been assured that someone—a future editor of my stories, perhaps—will be given the opportunity to record my last thoughts for posterity. Do not inquire how this letter will be preserved or eventually delivered; I do not understand the process myself. Suffice it to say that it will in due course be resurrected and published, and with it my standing as an author will be brought back to life—just like the dead dogs of Sardasa.

"For the record, I have been unable to reach the armies of Pancho Villa on this, my last journalistic assignment. Once I crossed into Mexico, I became progressively more confused. The last town I passed through was Ciudad Delicias, along the Rio Conchas in the state of Chihuahua. After that, I seemed to be traveling over the same ground every day, and yet the landmarks and guideposts were distinctly different. Finally, I collapsed in a fever of semi-exhaustion, wondering what would become of me.

"I did not have long to wait for an answer. Thunder heads began to gather on the horizon, and within half an hour, a terrible storm rolled over the Mexican hills toward me. I found cover in a small cave not far from where I had stopped to rest—a cave that turned out to be more than enough to protect me from one of the worst storms I have ever witnessed.

"For the next several hours, I believed that I had stumbled across a school for hell on earth. Lightning crashed everywhere around me; trees were uprooted and blown by the entrance of my protective shell. Rain fell by the tubfuls, washing away portions of the hillside on both sides of the cave. For a while, I thought my protective cave might easily become my tomb, but such was not the case. After four hours, the storm began to subside, and the sun shone once again.

"It was then that a most curious thing happened. A string of apparitions began to stroll up to the entrance of my cave, one following the other at discreet intervals. Each would pause and chat with me, then vanish into the atmosphere as the next took form. Yet even though they had no more substance than a ghost, they seemed to be made of flesh and blood; they were clearly not hallucinations.

"You may wonder how I can be so sure that

these dream images were not just figments of sunstroke compounded by the fierce display of the heavens I had just witnessed. I could not be certain of anything, except for one factor: every apparition that appeared happened to have been one of the characters in some story or another that I had written. They were my literary legacy.

"One by one they came, suddenly sprung to life: soldiers who had fought the Civil War of my imagination, husbands who had plotted to murder their wives, and an assortment of journalists, who slithered up to the cave on their bellies. It was a trifle disconcerting, I will admit, as I thought I had been done with every one of the motley gang. But once I recovered from my initial shock, I found the reunion invigorating. The implication, after all, was that these creations would outlive their creator in the minds and hearts of my readers—indeed, they had taken on a livingness that I could never have imparted.

"So, I joked and caroused with each character that chose to revisit me. They continued to come, in a fairly steady stream, until dusk began to gather on the horizon. Suddenly, I was aware of one final visitor, a tall pillar of light and motion that seemed to continually fade into the future.

"She identified herself as the goddess of Posterity.

" 'Have you achieved happiness, Ambrose?' the goddess asked.

" 'It is hard to believe that anyone could achieve happiness in a pit full of rattlesnakes,' I replied. 'But since I have had a career in which I could expose the snakes and shoot them, too—yes, I think I have been happy.'

" 'Do you have any regrets?' the goddess asked.

" 'My only regret is that my aim was not more true.' I replied.

" 'It is hard to hit a moving target,' she agreed.

" 'This is beginning to sound like an interview for either heaven or hell,' I said, suddenly projecting the drift of the questioning into the future.

" 'I am undecided what to do with you,' the goddess explained. 'Each person who comes to us must be judged. Most people are stuck in the present, and to the present return. A few are ready for Posterity, but that is a heavy burden to bear. The real question is: are you yet ready for Immortality?'

" 'I am sure I do not know,' I replied.

" 'In that, you are correct. No mortal can know. But nonetheless you must choose. I have three choices for you.

" 'You can be mugged by Mexcian bandits and left to die here in the Mexican highlands. You will shortly be forgotten, and nothing more will be heard of Ambrose Bierce. Or I could let you continue your present journey and join the armies of Pancho Villa, but if I do, you will be wounded by a stray bullet and die in the Mexican hills. Your publisher—'

" 'William Randolph Hearst? Do you know him?'

" 'A man who has brought untold misery to millions? Of course I know him. He will become infuriated and raise a private army to come down and teach Villa proper manners, thereby altering the course of history.'

" 'Oh,' I said with a sigh, perhaps realizing more profoundly than ever before the true power of the press. At the same time, I must admit a quick twinge of delight that Hearst would actually seek to revenge my death. In my heart, I knew it would just be to him an opportunity to sell papers, but the thought still gave me warmth and comfort—for a moment.

" 'Of all the options, the one I recommend is the third. The cave you have sought refuge in, the cave that has protected you from this storm, is actually the Cave of Posterity. It is a cave that can be found on every continent. To this cave, or the local duplicate of it, dozens of writers and artists have crawled throughout the centuries, begging to have their works and canvases blessed, so that they would never be forgotten by humanity."

" 'Do I need such a benediction?' I asked. 'After all, I am well known throughout the land. Just moments ago you said that the great Hearst himself would send a private army to avenge my death.'

" 'Yes, that is true. But even Hearst will not survive in the memories of mankind unless he pays tribute to the Cave of Posterity. In your case—well, let me show you what will happen.'

"The goddess unrolled a huge scroll containing

charts of everything I had done so far: what I had written, whom I had offended, duels I had fought, and much more. Then she unfurled the scroll a bit further, revealing a graph—with a decidedly downward trend. It was labeled 'Reputation of Ambrose Bierce.'

" 'Your reputation will be smeared first of all by the thousands of people who survived your habit of using them for target practice. What is left of it will then be turned over to the prudes and pious custodians of American culture, who will in particular avenge themselves for your treatment of one Thomas Dobsho.'

" 'That wasn't me playing those pranks!' I protested, perhaps a bit too vigorously. 'That was the persona I created for my stories. I'm just a peace-loving, retiring old codger.'

" 'A journalist,' the goddess reminded me. 'A beloved journalist working for William Randolph Hearst.'

" 'True,' I muttered, ashamed of my sins. 'Too true.'

" 'Not yet being dead, it would be impossible for you to know this, but you have indeed created a whole new species of journalist—the syndicated columnist.'

" 'A what?'

" 'A syndicated columnist—an especially ignorant sort of chap who will be allowed to infect the whole nation with three columns of perverse thinking per week. You have been the forerunner of this damnable bunch, but will not be remembered for it. Your contribution will be overshadowed by such writers as Walter Winchell, Damon Runyan, Jimmy Breslin, and Bob Greene.

" 'Getting back to the matter of your reputation, the little that is left of it once the prudes dispose of you will be effectively buried by the next few generations of school teachers and college professors, who consider themselves the judge and jury of English and American letters. They will kill you simply by not teaching you.'

" 'And why would they not teach me?'

" 'Did you ever read anything funny in school, or even anything mildly interesting?'

" 'Not that I can remember.'

" 'Exactly. Our literature is filled with wonderful stories and poems that are fun to read as well as great literature. But American professional academics are offended by the idea that learning could be fun. So they ignore anything that might want to make their students keep on reading, in favor of brown depressing stories about the loser class.'

" 'Loser class? Don't you mean the lower class?'

" 'Look, Ambrose, I am the goddess of Posterity. I know exactly what I mean.'

" 'No offense meant,' I mumbled.

" 'None taken, except by this deliberate effort of the schools to sabotage everything good and bright in literature. Which brings me to my point.

We think your stories need to be preserved. We would hate to see them lost.'

" 'So, what would you recommend?' I asked.

" 'The third option. Join with us, and we will guard your works against oblivion. We will cause them to fade from the public eye for seventy-five years or so, until all of your enemies and detractors die. Then, when the time is right, we will reintroduce them to a waiting reading public, so they can be properly adjudged.'

" 'And what happens to me?'

" 'You enjoy immortality. Your genius qualifies you to inspire other writers of a similar bent. You become a muse.'

" 'I'm not quite the right sex for that, am I?'

" 'I didn't say your physical form would become a muse—I said your genius would. And genius is both masculine and feminine. I myself am both,' the goddess said. 'Would you like to see my masculine nature?'

"I hastily assured her that it would not be necessary.

" 'It's just as well,' the goddess said with a sigh. 'The last time I made a sudden switch before mortal eyes, the whole population of Lesbos got hopelessly confused. In any event, you would not become a muse right away. You would go through training.'

" 'Training?'

" 'Posterity training—to learn what elements of

human genius are worth preserving, and what ought to be dumped in a trash can.'

" 'I think I have a pretty good idea of that already,' I suggested.

" 'You do. Anyone who can see as clearly as you into the vicious, mean, argumentative, jealous, fearful, vain, ambitious, and doubting organ of men and women that they euphemistically call a heart is a perfect candidate for the job. But your raw genius is colored by your own experiences and attitudes. It needs to be refined a bit—tweaked, as it were.'

" 'Tweaked?'

" 'That's right. Do you remember the story you wrote about the resurrection of dead dogs?'

"I nodded yes.

" 'Human civilization is filled with far too many dead dogs—the decaying carcasses of grandiose ideas and propositions that misled humanity instead of inspiring it. Your first job will be to learn to tell the difference between a dead dog of an idea and a living, breathing inspiration, then encourage writers and artists to deodorize the dead dog, as you so pungently put it, and encourage the use of the living, vital idea.'

" 'It sounds like a crusade against everything hackneyed and clichéd.'

" 'Oh, it's much more than just that,' the goddess insisted. 'You have heard of Marxism, have you not?'

" 'I am a journalist, Madam.'

" 'Well, between Marxism and capitalism, which is the dead dog and which is the living idea?'

" 'I am more aware of the faults of capitalism, of course, but I fail to see how Marxism could be workable. It's probably the dead dog.'

" 'Exactly!' the goddess beamed. "But it's going to take humanity ninety years of catastrophe and bloodshed to figure that out, even with a lot of deodorizing from us.'

" 'I am beginning to understand how great the need is. One whiff of the wrong idea, and humanity can be stuck on an erroneous tangent for decades!'

" 'Until the stench from the decaying carcasses becomes so great that they are forced to think straight. Ultimately, it is the work of artists and writers around the globe to teach the rest of humanity to tell the difference between a wholesome idea and a foul one.'

" 'Once I have learned to deodorize ideas, then what?' I asked.

" 'Whoa, there!' the goddess exclaimed. 'One step at a time. I can't give you a full tour of the next one thousand years. But you won't be disappointed.'

" 'Okay,' I said, 'I'm in. What happens next?'

" 'You need to write a final letter to posterity, which we will deliver to the right place at the proper time, when humanity has grown enough to more fully appreciate your writings. Then we will step through the doorway of the cave together, and leave this vale of suffering and woe. You shall become Immortal.'

"So there it is. This is a true record of all that has happened this day, the eighth of August of 1914, my final day on earth as a mortal being. I am about to depart on my new career, an apprentice deodorizer of dead dogs. The foul odors of original sin, existentialism, realism, the income tax, and phonetics already batter my sensitive nose. But I shall struggle onward, unbloodied, and appeal to all who might read this to do the same. It does not matter whether or not you are a writer or a reader, we all deal with ideas. Do not let the foul stench of dead ideas turn your own mind into a festering fen or hate campaign. Deodorize!"

"I bid you farewell. Ambrose Bierce."

Having finished reading the letter, I set it down. so moved that tears came to my eyes. Ambrose Bierce told some tall tales in his day, I thought, but this was a whopper! But what if it was? The point he made was important. Good literature and the arts are not just a huge pile of faggots upon which more and more stories and paintings are piled. The truly great works must be culled from the rest and preserved. Just so, the great living ideas of life must be culled from the stupid ones, and preserved.

The satires of Ambrose Bierce point out the stupid ideas that need to be deodorized. Whether they are or not is up to us.

Don't let dead dogs lie. Deodorize!

Want More Copies?

A Deodorizer of Dead Dogs makes a wonderful gift for anyone with a nose for what's going on in the world. Additional copies may be purchased at your favorite bookstore, or directly from the publisher.

Orders from the publisher can be made by calling Enthea Press toll free, 1-800-336-7769, and charging your order to MasterCard, VISA, Discover, Diners Club, or American Express. Or send a check for the full amount of your order plus shipping to Enthea Press, 4255 Trotters Way, #13-A, Alpharetta, GA 30004. Our e-mail address is light@stc.net.

The cost of one copy is $9.95 plus $3 for postage. The cost of 10 or more copies is $7 per book plus $4 postage per address. Call for prices on 25 or more copies.

Another book from Enthea Press:

FART PROUDLY

Writings of Benjamin Franklin You Never Read in School
Edited by Carl Japikse

A collection of the satirical and humorous writings of Benjamin Franklin, including his famous essay on farting, "A Letter to the Royal Academy." On sale for $8.95 at bookstores everywhere, or from Enthea Press (add $3 shipping).